The Orloj of Venice

The Orloj series: Vol. 2

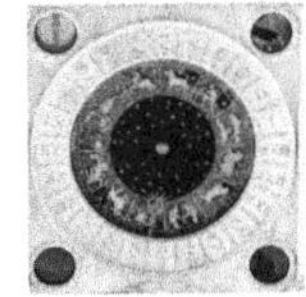

Erasmus Cromwell-Smith II

The Orloj of Venice
© Erasmus Cromwell-Smith II
© Erasmus Press

ISBN: ISBN: 978-1-7369968-6-7
Library of Congress Number: Case # 1-11019980984
Publisher: Erasmus Press
Editor: Elisa Arraiz Lucca
Co-Editor: Tracy-Ann Wynter
Proofreading: D. Suster, Tracy-Ann Wynter, Janet Bartos
Cover Design and Interior Design: Alfredo Sainz Blanco
www.erasmuscromwellsmith.com
First edition
Printed in USA, 2021.

<u>Books written by the author</u>

In English,	**En Español,**

<u>As Erasmus Cromwell-Smith II:</u>   *<u>Como Erasmus Cromwell-Smith II</u>:*

The Equilibrist series,	***La serie El Equilibrista,***
(Inspirational/Philosophical)	(Inspiracional/Filosófico)
-The Happiness Triangle (Volume 1).	-El triángulo de la felicidad (Volumen 1).
-Geniality (Volume 2).	-Genialidad (Volumen 2).
-The Magic in Life (Volume 3).	-La magia de la vida (Volumen 3).
-Poetry in Equilibrium (Volume 4).	-Poesía en equilibrio (Volumen 4).
(Young Adults)	(Jóvenes Adultos)
-The Orloj of Prague (Volume 5).	-El Orloj de Praga (Volumen 5).
-The Orloj of Venice (Volume 6).	-El Orloj de Venecia (Volumen 6).
-The Orloj of Paris (Volume 7).	-El Orloj de Paris (Volumen 7).
-The Orloj of London (Volume 8).	-El Orloj de Londres (Volumen 8).
-Poetry in Balance (Volume 9).	-Poesía en Balance (Volumen 9).

<u>As Erasmus Cromwell-Smith</u>   *<u>Como Erasmus Cromwell-Smith</u>*

The South Beach Conversational Method	*El Método Conversacional South Beach*
(Educational)	(Educacional)
- Spanish	- Inglés,
- German	- Alemán
- French	- Francés
- Italian	- Italiano
- Portuguese	- Portugués

The Nicolas Tosh Series, (Sci-fi)
- Algorithm-323 (Volume 1).
- Tosh (Volume 2).

<u>As Nelson Hamel (*)</u>

The Paradise Island Series, (Action/Thriller)
- Miami Beach, Paradise Island (Volume 1).
- Dangerous Liaisons: Miami Beach (Volume 2).
- The Rebel Hackers of Point Breeze (Volume 1), (Sci/fi).

(*) in collaboration with Charles Sibley.

All titles are or will be available in audio book.

Table of Contents

Glossary

"Characters"

-The Orloj.

-The Burly Man (The street version of The Orloj).

-Thumbpee.

-Buggie.

"The Six Harlequins"

- Erasmus Jr. aka BLUNT; blue clothes Boston, Mass. USA.
- Sofia aka REDDISH; red clothes, Barcelona, Spain.
- Sanjiv aka FIREE; orange clothes; Mumbai, India.
- Winnie aka CHECKERED; black & white clothes; Pretoria, South Africa.
- Sang-Chang aka BREEZIE; yellow clothes, Shanghai, China.
- Carole aka GREENIE; green clothes, Beirut, Lebanon.

"The Six Shepherd-Moors"
- Cornelius Tetragor, Shepherd-moor of Honesty; long white hair, ponytail, wears a long robe.
- Lazarus Zeetrikus, Shepherd-moor of Holding Grudges; a tall old man with a bent old hat.
- Lucrecia Van Egmond, Shepherd-moor of Perseverance and Grit; long white threaded hair, pale skim aquiline nose, milky blue eyes, fine features, ankle length skirt, long sleeve shirt.
- Paulina Tetrikus, Shepherd-moor of Loyalty; short and hunched, short fuse, avoid looking in the eye, beautiful but angry face, short black hair, green eyes.
- Morpheus Rubicom, Shepherd-moor of Betrayal; nervous, never sits still, puffy eyes, extremely skinny and tall, mat of wrangled curled hair, wears loose fitting, hanging clothes

- Lettizia Dillettante, Shepherd-moor of Forgiveness;
  blond hair on a ponytail, statuesque, self-aware but
  humble. A Nordic beauty with a Mediterranean
  name.

"Other Characters"
- Erasmus Sr. (Blunt's father).
- Victoria (Blunt's mother).
- Zbynek Kraus, the clock antiquarian. Long white hair in a
  ponytail, Fumanchu mustache, wears an electric blue
  robe and bent cone hat (both with stars and bolts).
- Bartholomeus, Roberto, and Maria Antonella (Blunt's
  uncle and aunt).
- Antonella D'Agostino & Leonardo Conti (Italian antiquarians).

"Clues Found"
- The crossing starts where you least expect it. But you'll only
  find it if you follow that what you've acquired in your
  quest. Only compassion will lead you to the Grand Canal.
- Trust not what you see but what you step into. The way
  forward will require a leap of faith from one of you. Once
  you all find who it is; trust and patience will be required.
- Perfect timing will be required but it will not be obvious to
  you all. The north star will be your guide but at times
  following it will challenge your better instincts.
- Sometimes you'll have to go up in order to go down and
  you will have to go right in order to go left and vice versa.
  Also, the path ahead of you at some point will be
  interrupted, it'll be entirely up to you to decide what is the
  best option ahead of you. Always remember, if you jump
  with intent, only a leap of faith will take you to the other
  side.
- The deep ends of the twirling waters hold a secret you must
  unveil. You'll have to conquer your fears to solve the
  riddle.
- There's a rainbow at the end of every trying and
  cumbersome path. Such reward will come to you only if
  you keep the end in sight and avoid getting sidetracked.

"Powers Earned"
- You now have the ability to see reality while in the presence and surrounded by fantasy. Thus, you won't be fooled easily by   it.
- You now have the ability to hover if the situation requires it. But for it to work you'll have to visualize it first. Ah! one more thing; only one of you at a time will be able to use this power.
- You guys now have the ability to breath under water.
- You all now have the power to become other people of your choosing with one caveat, it'll be on appearance only and not on a permanent basis, in fact it will only last for a short time.
- All of you now have the power to perceive what someone else is feeling. Use it wisely.
- This time you will be able to use your powers during your final quest on the bridge crossing.

"Questions posed on the Perseverance & Grit Challenge"
- Who is the flutist? (To Blunt).
- What does the piper mean to you? (To Reddish).
- What does the flutist represent to you? (To Greenie).
- How do you feel when encounter the flutist? (To Firee).
- The piper is a symbol of what to you? (To Breezie).
- The piper comes and goes like what? (To Checkered).
  The answer is the same for all:
  HAPPINESS!

Note by the Author,

In the preceding book "The Orloj of Prague," the magic ride went on like this...

The very first time I saw The Orloj from afar, across Prague's "Nove Mesto" (The Old Town Square); I felt an inexplicable and intense pull seizing me. It all took place on a European summer vacation -I was just twelve years old- while strolling along with my parents over the streets of the magical town.

My fascination with the ancient yet resplendent astrological clock led me into an alternate menacing world within the mysterious city of spires, where every year
over the course of a few days, a gathering of wizards, magicians, enchanters, conjurers, and witches from all over the world, takes place.

At the center of it all, the human form of a time exacting machine guided a group of five youngsters and me
- dressed at times as colorful harlequins (as in court jesters) - on a 24 hour- long journey to become wizard apprentices.

Throughout our quest, we were challenged to learn three essential human virtues and three perilous vices to avoid. To achieve this, we first had to find six statues
possessing them. Then, we were imparted with teachings by the statues, each one of them impersonating book antiquarians,

followed by our demonstration of the mastery of each virtue and vice. Every time we succeeded, we were granted a clue and a magical power.

The gigantic clock provided us with two guides: One called Thumbpee, claiming to be my conscience during our quest. He was spec of a man incessantly showing up, and then suddenly and annoyingly, vanishing again and again from my shoulder. The other we named Buggie, a tiny and noisy flying bug that steered us either with the intensity of the buzz from his flapping wings or with a miniature, but always timely green laser beam that the nagging bug pointed to lead us in the right direction. Eventually, it was a comforting revelation when we learned from The Orloj that our unruly, but very valuable guides, turned out to be his sons, the ancient watch's very own long and short hands, acting as our quest's compass.

With each of the clues and powers earned, we were able to overcome a string of non-stop seemingly impossible obstacles along Prague's Hradcany Castle's tunnel under the Vltava river. On each hurdle, we had to show our practical knowledge of each one of the virtues or flaws we'd learned. Throughout, our good judgment and common sense under extreme pressure and stress were tested.

Once we reached the other end, The Orloj was waiting for us at the castle's doorstep. Soon after, at the adjacent National Library (also known as the Klementinum), he rewarded us with our credentials as wizard apprentices. Then, he extended an invitation to continue our apprenticeship the following year, on the same dates, same wizards, magicians, enchanters, conjurers, and witches' gathering but at a different and intriguing new location.

In the story to follow, the human version of The Orloj inhabits the San Marco Square astrological clock in Venice. The narrative delves into the adventure that takes place the following summer. Once again, the six of us are led by the eccentric time measuring device. This time our goal is to become fully accredited young wizards.

Everything begins in the same place as last year, the institute where I teach...

Erasmus Cromwell-Smith II
Written in T.D.O.K in 2057.

PREFACE

Presidio
San Francisco Bay Area (Fall of 2056)

From the shoreline, the kiting sails seem to brush the crest of the lazy wave. The lanky surfer gathers speed as the sun starts to break. He heads straight into the next undulating wave. Riding it up as a ramp, he's catapulted into a cloudless sky: 20, 30, 40 feet high. As he climbs, an upper easterly wind gust lifts him even further and for an instant with the rectangular sail acting as his own pair of wings, he seems to hover above the city. At least that's how he feels contemplating the magnificent hilly town and the Bay area with its picture-perfect Golden Bridge and even its tiny landmark, Alcatraz Island, gorgeous from afar, yet regrettable up close with painful laments crying out through the walls.

When Erasmus Cromwell-Smith II heads to the shore, Laureen Tabernaki has just finished kiting ahead of him. The moment she's off the water her usual uncontrollable shivering begins. The thick neoprene suit, hood, and boots -without the adrenaline rush and physical exertion- are no defense against the bay's wind and cold water.

"How was it?" He says while walking off the cold bay waters, board in hand.

Unable to answer, her arms wrapped around her body, she shakes uncontrollably while her lips tremble. The young professor drops his board and embraces his on-and-off girlfriend for the last 2 years. Arms around her, he walks his other half to her electric SUV parked 100 yards away. He leads her to the driver's seat then turns the heater on at full blast.

"My brave Vesuvian," he says caressing her cheeks.

She smiles back faintly at him. Closing the door, he goes back to rinse and fold both their sails. He then washes the 2 boards before storing everything in the back of the 4-wheeler.

"It was awesome!" She says with a frail voice, while lowering the window,

He smiles back as he dismounts his mountain bike from the vehicle's roof rack then pulls from the back seat a large sac with shoulder straps.

"Off to class my lady," he says as he contorts taking off his wetsuit and replacing it with baggy sweatpants and a shirt.

"I don't know how you can wear fresh new clothes over saltwater."

"I'll rinse it off before I ride the Hyperloop," Erasmus replies as he packs his sack with 2 layers of clothes: thermal and wool.

He walks out and around the driver's window.

"Have a fantastic day my love," he says planting a noisy kiss on her mouth.

"I have to be in Cupertino before 9am," she replies. "What are you taking? He asks as he mounts his bike.

"The self-flying drone," she says referring to the shape of the latest flying contraption to hit the market, "I hate it though. It's a quick, but a windy and cold ride. Twice freezing on a single morning is too much for me," she says as her whimsical free-spirited pedagogue pedals away.

Hyperloop Station
Downtown, San Francisco (Fall of 2056)

After a quick shower in the public baths of the station, fully dressed as his usual eccentric-self the spirited professor -bike in hand- boards the windowless cabin with the shape of an oversized gel pill. Moments later, in a near-vacuum state, levitating -as if on a hockey table effect- Cromwell-Smith travels at just short of 500 mph inside of a tube over an elevated monorail line. Front air inducting engines virtually eliminate the wind shear that occurs at those speeds. He feels like he's inside one of those pneumatic tubes at the drive-in bank-teller window.

'The principle is the same,' he mulls over as he contemplates the scrolling landscape -synchronized with their speed- projected in high-resolution virtual reality images on the cylindrical walls of the cabin. It takes him just a few minutes to traverse 150 miles.

"The Central Institute of Arts and Literature (Fall of 2056)

Professor Cromwell-Smith II leisurely rides his bike for 15 minutes from California's Central Valley hyperloop station to the university campus. Dressed from head to toe in pastel green denim, back-pack on his shoulder; his mountain bike duly parked, he walks with ease into the faculty building.

A short text message notification from Laureen vibrates tactically on his watch, confirming she's made it on time to her office.

"ME2 LOV ECS," is his cursory reply.

When he walks into class with care-free strides, he's 3 minutes late, as he usually is. The auditorium is packed. The new semester's first day of class always feels like it is supercharged with positive energy. An intense buzz can be felt throughout the class. Countless personal communication devices -many with holographic images floating in the air- can be seen in front of the mesmerized students. Numerous over-sized screens in front of the stage show images of packed classrooms across the nation's dominions. There are 13,500 attendees, 500 of which are in his presence, and 13,000 attending via a live web link.

As the students see him enter the auditorium, the virtual screens and personal communications devices all disappear within seconds. They all know better what his expectations are.

"How's everyone today?"

"Awesome!"

"I hope you all had a great summer."

He scans the crowd and sees eager and expectant faces across the audience.

"In this course, we'll continue right where we left off last year. My second adventure with an astrological clock in Europe began like this...

INTRODUCTION

The winds blow, swirl and buzz uncontrollably. Menacing clouds are gathering at full speed! Lightning strikes the skies with blinding flashes of light. Thunder deafens as it explodes in a row. Air currents collide in a Cumulus-Nimbus cloud. The dark and hidden forces of the world of magic spread across an increasingly gray sky. An evil spirit, a detestable figure, a deceitful being, insignificant in stature and yet full of evil intentions, surrounds me. His spirit mixes with the storms as he waits impatiently for the arrival of the new crop of magicians-in-training. His only goal is to make us fail. He wants to interrupt and end our quest and adventure as we visit the ancient city of Europe, the enchanting and mysterious enclave of Venice. Fortunately for us there's a magical melody and an inspired Piper who appears when good things happen.

HAY -ON- WYE (Summer of the year 2031)
Wales, UK

Growing up in Boston hasn't made it easy for a Yank (Yankee) like me to adjust to the "City of Books," as my father's birthplace, Hay- On-Wye, is known. My parents and I are living here temporarily so that I can experience the same world of old books that surrounded my dad in his childhood and adolescence. Lately though, I've been more interested in things to do with magic and witchcraft than life, which means my obsession has been at the expense of my family and school performance.

Recently I can only think about my next trip in the summer when I will meet the Orloj again. I've spent countless hours trying to use the powers I acquired in Prague, but I haven't been able to create portals or render myself invisible, much less stick to walls or vertical surfaces with my limbs. It's a total waste of time; my apprentice magician powers have abandoned me.

I talk to my father on a daily basis expressing my frustration, but there's not much he can do as he's not a wizard, warlock, or sorcerer. Naturally, he has no idea about the dark and occult forces of the world of magic either.

As part of my preparation, I decided to visit my bookseller mentor, Mr. Winston Wildenkoss, an antiquarian of books from Hay-on-Wye and an expert on the subject of magic. This is how one afternoon walking through the streets of my father's hometown, I pass in front of innumerable bookstores of old books, for which the town is world famous. When I turn the corner, I find the sign for his bookstore:

"Wildenkoss, Old Books on Magic"
(Established a long time ago)

I cross the street excitedly, but I'm stopped in my tracks by the sound of a small explosion that is more of a "PUFF!" than a bag. It's a noise that seems to be muffled by a silencer. I barely recover from the initial shock when a cloud of twinkling stardust shoots out of Mr. Wildenkoss's bookstore. I walk with quick steps towards the bookstore. I go in to make sure the owner is okay. I hesitantly enter but I can hardly see anything. A dust of small stars fills the air of the bookstore making it difficult to see.

"Vacrumdesidrium," says a familiar voice that speaks as if casting a spell. In an instant Winston Wildenkoss electric blue beret sucks up all the stardust. I remain near the front door, dumbfounded.

"Apprentice wizard, come in, I was waiting for you," he tells me.

My astonished eyes meet his as I shyly approach him.

"You may be wondering what kind of phenomenon has just occurred in these places," he says, demonstrating his observant vein.

I nod my head without taking my eyes off his gaze.

"What you heard, and saw was the end of an argument between an ungrateful sorcerer and his servant, an old-school mage.

"Are you a magician?"

"Of course, I am, and I'm afraid a very bad-tempered one. What you just witnessed was simply the final act in a dispute between wizards. They all end with a DANG! I apologize, but last year I couldn't tell you, since at that time you weren't yet a wizard's apprentice," he finishes with a mischievous look.

"How do you know about Prague?"

"Because I'm part of the worldwide organization of wizards, warlocks, and sorcerers. The so-called Fraternity.

"You were there? "

"Of course, I'm there every year."

"Do you know about any of our adventures?"

"I think so, many of us did them, in fact what you did was a true adventure. "

"Do you have any advice for me?"

"I can't give you any, you have to solve everything by yourself, but what I do have is a very special letter for you. I contemplate the old man with his long white beard, his intense blue eyes the same color as his beret and his electric blue jacket sprinkled with comets, planets, and stardust. My mentor turns the pages of the huge book with his pointed finger, the smell of old paper and leather permeating the air.

"Nothing is as it seems"

"Beware of anything that appears to be a certain way as it may be something totally different, even the opposite of what you think it is. Pay close attention to everything that seems to be the truth and be on guard against everything that seems real at first sight. Watch your feelings.

When you speak, use your common sense and good judgment, as the truth is difficult to discern.

When this is assailed by so many artifices, they're the only way we can jump into action, move forward, and execute, leaving things behind while at the same time walking the path of true realism so it's healthy to remember that what matters is not what it appears to be but the truth and nothing more."

Wildenkoss looks at my confused look and smiles. I know that he can't say a single word to guide me on my adventure in Venice.

"Young Erasmus, in due time you'll make use of the contents of this text. I wish you all the best in the challenge that lies ahead in Italy," he tells me. "There you will find what happens when things are not what they seem to be, in other words, the opposite of what you have just learned. In particular you will learn what to do when faced with the absurd and heinous." He adds.

"Now that you're a fledgling member of the Fraternity, there are many more things we can share in the near future," says the antiquarian Wildenkoss cryptically.

I hug him and thank him for everything.

I walk home slowly as I have a lot to think about. Even though I don't understand half of what the antiquarian said, I have learned since Prague to be patient when I don't understand everything. Eventually and inexorably, it will all make sense. Meanwhile, my excitement continues to grow. At home, my parents are already packing for the early train, I still have one stop to make before heading to Venice. The three of us travel to my hometown of Boston where we're going to visit my Aunt Sarah, who just had a set of twin girls. After this I will head to Italy while my parents embark on one of their usual summer trips around the world, I'll be joining them right after my trip to Venice.

Chapter 1
In Search of the Orloj

Malpensa International Airport (Summer of 2031)
Milan, Italy

J ust after my 13th birthday, my uncle Bartholomeous and I arrive to Italy early on a summer Sunday morning. The halls of Milan's Malpensa airport are empty as we seem to be the first on the ground from an avalanche of flights about to arrive from America. We hurry through the terminal eager to clear customs and immigration before other passengers arrive. I am excited to have my uncle by my side. This is my very first journey without my parents. So, being with whom I consider both my big brother and mentor makes me feel safe and confident. Besides, he's the only person in my family and circle of friends to know the truth about what happened to me
during the last summer in Prague.

"Well, well, well. Erasmus, you are one step closer to your second encounter with The Orloj," Bartholomeous says as we clear Italian immigration in a couple of minutes.

I say nothing but just continue to smile. I'm content with my circumstances while remembering last year's adventure. In anticipation, I taste the thrills of the adventure about to happen again.

"Hello, knock, knock. Anybody home? Where in the world are you Erasmus?"

"I just can't wait to get there Uncle Bart," I blurt out

distractedly, still thinking ahead of the moment.

"Getting there is not enough my absent-minded nephew. You need to figure out how to get inside the clock first. If we judge by the events in Prague, just standing in front of the clock won't be quite enough.

"I know uncle, I know. In Prague, Mr. Kraus' store was the portal.

"Young Erasmus, that happened because Kraus propitiated your entrance into the other Prague once you demonstrated your immutable enthusiasm for The Orloj," my uncle reflects with absolute accuracy.

When we exit into the arrival's hall, my Italian uncle Roberto Marcello, and my aunt Maria Antonella -both from my father's side- are waiting for us with big wide smiles.

"Bien Venuti! (welcome)" they say in unison as they hug and kiss both of us, with typical Italian hospitality.

As we spend the next hour exchanging anecdotes and pleasantries, it quickly becomes obvious to me that my uncle Bart was right all along. Despite my stubborn refusal for months to do so, his words were prophetic. "Erasmus, you've been postponing the inevitable. Soon after our arrival to Italy, you'll be forced to bring your uncle and aunt up to date about what happened to you in Prague. You'll have no choice especially if you need them and I suspect you will."

Predictably the conversation takes a U-turn, while we drive into Milan out of the blue, I start to explain to my Italian aunt and uncle what took place in Prague.

"Erasmus, what happened to your fellow harlequins?" My aunt asks when I am done.

(Reddish)
Barcelona, Spain (2031)

Sofia Alejandra Alonso Casal (aka Reddish) celebrates her 13th birthday, first on social media then with her family. As an only child, she's accustomed to being by herself or among her web friends. Both her parents being important members of Barcelona's Philharmonic orchestra, her father Rafael being the lead pianist and her mother being the leading violinist, Sofia has grown up traveling the world accompanying them on their world tours. With chestnut hair, caramel eyes and tall for her age, she's an avid reader, highly opinionated, loud, and hyper; hence, she couldn't be more different than both her parents. That's how her insistence on going to Venice during the summer lasts months, all to no avail until the Barcelona orchestra's schedule comes to her rescue. Concerts in Milan around the dates Sofia wishes to be in Venice solve the impasse and peculiar desire of their young daughter.

'If only they knew the adventure, I was part of, the previous summer,' she mulls over as she reads the credentials she earned in Prague as a wizard apprentice.

Her certificate bears the name Reddish. She chuckles at the sight of her other name. The one that no one knows about. 'If only they knew,' she repeats to herself once more, remembering with a sense of nostalgia, her exciting adventure, 'now I have to figure out how to get inside The Orloj and into the alternate Venice,' she reflects with a hint of anxiety bursting inside as she has no clue yet, how to achieve this.

Milan, Italy (Summer of 2031)

I am once more lost in my own thoughts and the memories of my experiences with the Orloj.

"Erasmus, did you hear your aunt's question about what happened to your fellow harlequins after Prague?" My uncle Bart asks.

"Absent-mindedness runs in the family," states Maria Antonella in jest.

Her words finally bring me back to earth.

"We never exchanged any info about each other, and we parted ways so quickly. I believe we were all so transfixed and in awe about everything we'd just experienced, that we simply forgot, and by the time we realized the omission, the six of us were already back with our families."

"You have no way to contact them?" Asks my aunt.

"No."

"A pity because the six of you are facing the same challenge of how to reach The Orloj once more," states my aunt.

My uncle Roberto has not said a word after I related The Orloj story, but that's about to change. First, he addresses my uncle Bartholomeous. "Bart, ever since you announced the trip with young Erasmus, it sounded cryptic and mysterious. Although my sister has always been into all kinds of dungeons and dragons' games and fantasies, I never have. So, if you all forgive me, I'm going to disembark your magic train at this time," he announces shortly before he parks in what I learn later is his place of residence, an immaculate condominium on a fashionable Milan neighborhood.

"Young Erasmus, I hope to spend some quality time with you before you leave. If you need me while you are at it, just buzz me and I'll come right away. Nevertheless, you're in good hands with your aunt Marian Antonella and your uncle Bart."

As he leaves my aunt takes the wheel and I sit next to her.

"He'll come around. Roberto is an architect, very abstract in his thinking and not very inclined to fantasies much less wizards," my aunt explains as soon as we are back on the road again.

"Where are we heading?" I ask.

"First, we are going to Florence to visit Leonardo Conti at his antique bookstore. He's an old friend of your father and a close associate of my mother. We have to research and quiz him about which -among Venice's antique bookstores- could be your portal into The Orloj and who could be the antiquarian that initiates you into your second quest," she says as we speed away on the Italian autostrada (highway).

(Breezie)
Shanghai, China (2031)

Sang-Chang Lin looks several years younger than his 13 years of age. He moves with ease through the crowd. At lunch hour the narrow streets of "old" Shanghai are packed with tourists and locals. The corner-tips of the red pagoda roofs are so close to each other that they seem to touch each other. Compared to the countless glass towers of the newer parts of the city, the ancient Chinese architecture of the old town always makes him feel comfortable and at home. Short for his age with a mane of straight-laced hair and tiny round rim glasses, all of it gives Sang-Chang the look of an impossibly young bookish boy. Right after finishing his morning middle-school session, he bolts out of the door and heads to meet with Jack Zhou at the antique bookstore his mentor's owned for five decades, right at the center of old Shanghai.

"Sir, I'm stuck and still cannot figure out how to access The Orloj in Venice," he asks Mr. Zhou as he sits facing him.

"Sang-Chang, dear boy, perhaps you're not asking yourself the right question."

"Mr. Zhou, I believe that last summer, my adventure with The Orloj happened by accident."

"Perhaps not. How did you know which place you needed to go to gain access to the living clock?"

"That's precisely my problem. I didn't know; I just went to an antique bookstore and the antiquarian sent me through a portal into an alternate version of the city of Prague."

"Sang-Chang! You are still not answering my question. Why did you go to that store? Why did he send you through the portal to see The Orloj?"

Obfuscated, Sang-Chang at first cannot think clearly. Perhaps he doesn't want to. Suddenly, something clicks, and his eyes begin to sparkle.

"I went to his store and met him because I was fascinated by the clock. I asked around who could tell me more about the ancient watch. Several people gave me the same reply," he explains in excitement to his mentor, "I was told that the antiquarian that knows the most about The Orloj in Prague is Mr. Kraus, the world-famous book antiquarian."

"And once you met him, why did he send you through the portal?"

Sang-Chang chuckles at the premonition that the riddle is finally solved, "because of my fascination and enthusiasm to learn everything about The Orloj."

"Realize mentee, the place to go in Venice is not a random location. To get to it you know now that first of all you have to ask and find out who is the foremost expert in town about the San Marco Square astrological clock. Once with him or her, you have to demonstrate your keen interest for the clock."

"Thank you, mentor Zhou."

"I recommend that before meeting with book antiquarians, you visit and study well the San Marco square watch."

"Will do," Sang-Chang replies casually as he storms out rushing to make it on time to his afternoon class. He's eager and itching to become Breezie -the harlequin- once more.

Conti Libri Antichi
(Conti Antique Bookstore) Florence, Italy
(Summer of 2031)

For several hours we've been searching and literally digging information about Venice antiquarians when the jet lag finally hits me. As I start yawning, Leonardo Conti, a long- time friend, and collaborator of my father, hands me the list.

"Erasmus, here are all the known Venice antiquarians. You have a list containing those in existence and those that are no longer in business." There it is, on a single piece of paper, the entire roster. Those antiquarians that aren't open any longer took him the longest to compile. Then, I see it and my eyes grow in size and intensity in an instant.

"What is it young man?" Asks Conti.

"Kraus' shop."

"What about it? It's been closed for more than a hundred years."

"It can't be."

"Why?"

"My parents and I were at Mr. Kraus' store in Prague last year."

"The store bears his name?"

"Yes."

"Maybe he's a descendant or a relative of the owner of the Kraus store in Venice. Let me check the Prague directory of antique bookstores, Kraus's is one that is actually very well indexed and always kept up to date."

He pages through a computer list and with a circumspect face he announces the startling news, "there's no store with that name in Prague. At least in last year's directory."

I look at him totally confused.

"Let me check something else," he says while delving in the same old books where he found the Venice book antiquarians no longer in business. Once more he spends a long time searching.

"There it is, Kraus Antiquarians, Prague. It closed its doors also more than a hundred years ago. Seems like the Venice and Prague stores were owned by the same antiquarian, a man called Znynek Kraus.

(Checkered)
Pretoria, South Africa (2031)

Young Minnie Mubate and her family couldn't feel prouder. At just 13 years of age, Minnie is the youngest of the countrywide-famous Pretorian choir. Today, in the city's main hall the chorus performs to a full house. Right in the middle of a magnificent rendering of "Panis Angelicus" she struggles to remain focused on the music notes and lyrics. Her mind is somewhere else. What she's been obsessing about for months is finally clear in her mind.

"Congratulations! We're all so proud of you," are the enthusiastic words she gets from her parents as they effusively hug and kiss her backstage, right after the group performance is over.

The precocious soprano, tall for her age, wears her hair crew-cut. Besides her gigantic gold-rimmed earrings, she dresses like every other teenager her age around the world, jeans, t-shirt, and sneakers. Her college-professor parents are the only people in the world that are privy to her previous summer adventure and are equally eager to find out what's on her mind.

"Dad, Mom. I'm now Checkered, the wizard apprentice."

"We are aware of that dear. Your certificate spells it clearly."

"Mom, being a wizard apprentice means that simply asking around town in Venice, as I did last year in Prague, regarding who is the most knowledgeable person about the San Marco astrological clock isn't going to be enough. This time I'll have to use wizardry in some form or fashion to get to The Orloj."

The Mubate family smiles together at the realization that Winnie has in all likelihood begun to solve the riddle. Now they're all looking forward to their upcoming trip to Italy where Minnie will be enrolled in a soprano's school for the whole summer except for a short break she'll take with her parents to visit the fabled city of Venice.

Venice, Italy

D'Agostino Antique Bookstore (2031)

The sun is setting as we cross the bridge onto the island of Venice. A city where water channels replace streets and gondolas replace vehicles, where the doorstep of renaissance palaces, stores, chapels, hotels even restaurants, end at the water's edge. A citadel that at some point in time was the center of Europe and consequently holds immense treasures of art and literature; exquisite and magnificent architectural jewels, endless labyrinths, dead ends, walkways, corners, and countless narrow and arched bridges that are all tiny and tight, filled with romance and beauty, timeless colors and design, incomparable taste and gusto but above all incomprehensively exposed and in peril to water, in particular to the "Aqua Alta" (The sporadic super- high tide).

I am filled with excitement to finally arrive at the place of my second adventure. Deep inside, I'm dying to get started. Yet I'm well aware that before anything else I need to solve the riddle of how to get to The Orloj.

My Italian aunt's mom, Antonella D'Agostino waits for us at the entrance to her store. Once more effusive hugs and kisses follow in typical Italian fashion.

"Young man, you're all grown-up. A bello ragazzi (a beautiful boy)," she says with full of enthusiasm, "tell me Erasmus how are your parents?" "Fine thank you."

I try my best to look distracted as we enter her impeccable store.

"Bart, you look so much like your mother, so handsome," she says kissing both of Bart's cheeks.

A bit embarrassed he mulls over, 'not bad for an 86-year old lady.'

For a long time, she was involved in a long-term relationship with my father. Roberto and Maria Antonella were born out of it. My father only learned about their existence long after their relationship had ended, and they were both full grown-up adults. Mrs. D'Agostino, an antiquarian herself along with her long- time business partner Mr. Conti, was also a close collaborator to my father's endeavors into the world of antique books. Hugs and kisses follow with typical Italian enthusiasm.

"How are your parents, Erasmus?"

"Fine," I reply distracted as we enter her impeccable store.

"Well, young Erasmus, or should I say, wizard apprentice?" She says with a wink. "Roberto has brought me up to date. Let me apologize for his behavior," she begins to say but it is interrupted by Uncle Bart.

"No need to. He was a gracious host and before we departed, Roberto was honest and blunt."

"After we left him, we went to see your partner, antiquarian Conti."

"Conti called me as well," Mrs. D'Agostino says. Then right away the dynamic lady is all action "Let's get to work then, shall we? Let me see the Venice antiquarian's directory Conti prepared please."

I hand it to her.

After reviewing it carefully. She returns it to me. "Kraus the book antiquarian you want to find, right?"

"Right."

"Then I'll take you over there myself."

"Ok let's go over there then."

"But hasn't he been out of business for more than a century?"

"I won't comment anything further about who you're after. Follow me please," cryptically she says.

We walk slowly out of her store following the old grand dame and help her board in the same gondola that brought us in. "The Gondolieri" (driver) takes us to the address of Mr. Kraus' store. We slow down in front of a fashion-design shop.

"This is it," Mrs. D'Agostino says pointing to the store in front of us. We all look incredulously at her.

"Sorry, it's been gone for a long time Erasmus, sorry," she says.

I step out and look at the faded pastel blue and yellow facade of what in reality is the renovated structure of an old Venetian palace.

"Look," I say excitedly, pointing it out to them. Slightly to the side of the shop's front wall, almost invisible to the eye, the old hand-painted sign hasn't been entirely deleted. My aunt, Maria Antonella, is as surprised as me as she reads aloud the old store name that still faintly visible, "Zbynek Kraus, Antique Books Shop for the Dark Arts and Occult Sciences."

In the meantime, I have a sick feeling in my stomach. "The store doesn't really exist anymore," I realize, now totally lost.

(Firee)
Bangalore, India (2031).

Sanjiv Kalwani is a computer whiz at 13. Raised in a tech environment, his father is a project manager at a software development company. His mother is an executive at a call-center enterprise that provides customer service support for electronic goods manufacturers in the North American market.

The young boy has been surrounded by the latest gadgets and electronics ever since he can remember. He's lanky and elongated in stature for his age, with intense yellowish eyes, curly brown hair that covers her forehead, and double rimmed giant glasses to make up for his short slightness. His obsession for the last six months has been to locate his five fellow harlequins that shared the Prague adventure during the previous year. Sanjiv's has searched and searched through the web to find them. But having nothing but their first names, country, city of residence; and as him all of the harlequins being just kids, all of his efforts have been in vain. As the date of going back to his annual summer camp ritual in Switzerland, -Firee- as he was called in Prague, finds himself completely unprepared for his planned visit to Venice right at the end of his European trip. Not only is he empty-handed as far as the identities of his fellow wizard apprentices but perhaps more troublesome, he has no idea how he's going to be able to locate The Orloj this time around, much less how is he going to find the portal to cross into Venice's alternate world.

D'Agostino Antique Bookstore
Venice, Italy (2031).

The moment the gondola drops us right back in front of Mrs. D'Agostino's store, I decide to call my father, retired professor Erasmus Cromwell-Smith Sr.

"Dad?" I say while I place him on the speakerphone.

"Erasmus dear, how are you?" Replies my mother Victoria Emerson-Lloyd.

"Hi mom, I am doing just fine," I lie badly. "Mom, can I talk to dad?" I ask trying to avoid a deeper or longer conversation with her.

"Junior, you sound disturbed," says my father speaking with his usual thunderous voice, thick with the purest of British accents.

Mrs. D'Agostino, my aunt Maria Antonella and my uncle Bart are also all listening attentively through a speakerphone as well.

"Kraus the antiquarian doesn't exist,"

"Son, explain yourself," solemnly demands my father.

"Both antiquarian registers in Prague and Venice state that the place closed more than a hundred years ago."

"But Erasmus dear, we all met him last year. We were at his store. Your father corresponded with him in advance to set up the appointment. Right dear?" My mother rambles.

"Indeed, I did, let me recall how it was? Oh yeah, we connected through the phone."

"Do you have his number dad?"

"Yes, let me look for it. I've got it. Let me dial him up with your mom's phone," he says as he dials in the numbers.

"Dobri Noce," is the female voice we all hear on the other end.

"That's goodnight in Czech," my father explains. "Do you speak English?" He asks.

"Yes, a little," she says with a heavily accented English.

"Can I speak with antiquarian Kraus?"

"Who?"

"Zbynek Kraus, the antiquarian." Silence ensues.

"Sir, there's no Zbynek Kraus in here. This is a wizardry museum. The gentleman you refer to, used to have an antique Bookstore on these premises. But that was more than... well, a long, long time ago. The old master wizard has been dead for more than a hundred years. This museum honors him among other great sorcerers.

(Greenie)
Beirut, Lebanon (2031)

Only 13 years old, Carole Jamal, known as Greenie the green Harlequin in Prague the previous summer, is the most famous child actress in Lebanon. She's of average
height with blond curly hair, and blue eyes. She's the lead character in the country's most popular TV program for viewers aged 8-12. A foursome of young adventurers that embark on thrilling treks and journeys to the outdoors as part of a teen patrol of explorers of their nation's backcountry and mountain terrain. More than a million viewers tune in every week to follow her TV sitcom. As both of her parents were actors as well, from an early age, Carole was predestined to follow their footsteps. Her upcoming summer trip to Italy, including Venice, has only been confirmed recently as her TV shooting schedule had to be
literally halted for a couple of weeks during her absence.

"Mom, Dad, for the first time I've figured out some of my skills as a wizard apprentice. I already know how to find antiquarian Kraus in Venice," Carole says smiling from ear to ear.

Chapter 2
La Serenísima
(The Most Placid City)

Venice, Italy (2031)
D'Agostino Antique Bookstore

Both my parents in Boston and the four of us in Venice look at the Google maps image of Prague's wizardry museum, the same building where my parents and I met Mr. Kraus last year. What we visited though was not a museum, but an antique book shop specializing in the dark and occult arts.

"Junior, zoom the image to the small bronze plaque." As I do my, parents and I are left speechless. It says...

"Prague's Wizardry Museum (founded 100 years ago)"

"But, we were there," says my mother.

"This is all absurd," my father says.

"There's something magic in all of this," I say.

"Why?" Asks my uncle Bartholomeous.

"Notice, there's something that does not make sense with the sign, it reads... founded 100 years ago! In other words, according to the sign, each and every day forward, the museum will always be founded 100 years ago."

"Dad, Mom, I've got to go. Thanks. I'll let you know what happens. I'm taking uncle Bart and Aunt Maria Antonella with me."

"Be careful son," my mom says.

"Love you," they both say happily in unison.

"Love you too," I reply with urgency in my voice.

"Mrs. D'Agostino…"

"Call me Antonella, please."

"Mrs. Antonella, are there any antique bookstores in Venice, specialized in wizardry?" I ask.

"We have one called Antique Wizardry Books; it's been around for the last twenty years. Let me get you the directions on how to get there."

"Thank you so much. But first I'm going to take a look at the St. Marco Square's clock," I say.

Before parting ways, I hug and kiss Mrs. D'Agostino on both cheeks. My grateful smile is all she needs to wave us off with absolute joy on her face.

After another short gondola ride, the three of us disembark in the fabled San Marco Square. We walk across the "piazza" (square) towards its astrological clock which is built in a small tower.

"I need a local guide that can answer a few questions about the clock," I say aloud.

No sooner had I finished saying it when a peculiar solution strolls right in front of us. Wearing a long salty beard, dark sunglasses, a dog, and a cane to aid him, a blind old man passes by. The sign he carries is music to my ears…

"Do you want to know more about the San Marco Square Clock? Hire me! I speak English, German, French and a bit of Spanish."

I immediately do and with the exuberance of my age, I pay him right away in cash. I react so quickly that my aunt and uncle don't have time to say anything, so they just contemplate me with bemused faces.

"Signore, what can you tell us about the clock?"

"Let's see what we have here. By the age, accent, and tone of your voice, I gather an inquisitive American youngster, am I right?"

"Yes." I respond slowly hesitating but impatient, nevertheless.

"Let's see, the San Marco Square Astrological Clock was built at the end of the 15th century. It was officially inaugurated on February 1, 1497, in other words in the middle of the 15th century. Although, its concentric- ring dials marked the positions of five planets, as well as the moon phases, the sun's position in the Zodiac as well as a 24-hour day in Roman numerals; almost three centuries later, the concentric-ring planet dials were replaced by a rotating Moonball to mark the moon phases. The Roman numerals were replaced by Arabic numerals marking a day measured in 12-hour cycles. The clock has a massive bell and two bronze Shepherd-Moors statues, each 2.5 meters high. They strike the bell with mallets in six groups of 22 blows at 12:00 and 0:00 hours. The clock also has a carousel that shows "the Procession of the Magi," which is announced by an angel blowing a trumpet," the blind man says.

As he finishes, I hear the clock bell ringing. At least I believe I do because the fact is that the mallets of the bell- ringing Shepherds are not moving. For a brief moment, it seems as if the clock's carousel is moving. But as I look closer, I realize that in reality that it isn't moving either. There's something else moving through it though. It's green in color. Wait a minute. Is that Greenie, Carole from Lebanon, my green harlequin buddy back in Prague? She turns her head ever so slightly. Is she staring at me? Then as quickly as she arrives, she's gone. It all happened in an instant. Instinctively,

I turn around and quickly observe my aunt and uncle; they are totally unaware.

"Sometimes people see strange figures in the clock," says the blind old man. His words jolt me, "how does he know?" I ask aloud.

"Knows what?" Asks my aunt.

The blind old man shrugs his shoulder and smiles. Then I get it.

"Sir, are there any mysteries surrounding the clock? What else can you tell us about it?" I ask.

"Ragazzi (Young Man), call me Signore Lucciano."

"Ok, no problem will do."

"What else would you like to know?" He asks.

"Signore Lucciano, anything out of the ordinary. Any legends. Any curses. There has to be more. I sense it."

"Well, ragazzi, you are a very curious and persistent young man. Tell you what; let the four of us have a seat at the street cafe around the corner."

At first sight, there isn't any, but we all follow him. Sure enough, when we exit the Piazza on the left side of an adjacent little street, the fresh aroma of fresh coffee and the buzzing activity of the Italian baristas at work makes itself present. Then it happens; that's when I see them for the first time in Venice. A couple of translucent figures in the balconies of the narrow street.

"Is that the bubbly boy from Prague?" says one of the transparent creatures. "One that I've seen before with a front tooth missing and dressed like a ragged dirty old pirate. "What is it that we concluded in Prague; is it that he's a daddy's boy or a mommy's boy?" he asks the second figure, "Where's your mommy? And where's your daddy?" He continues.

"Oh! The blue harlequin boy. He's now a wizard apprentice. What a joke! But look at his face. He's totally lost. Perhaps he's not going to make it on time to the Venice wizard festivities this year," says an old transparent woman dressed like a tavern waitress, continuing the ruse.

I glance at my aunt and uncle and just like it happened in Prague with my parents, they have no clue what's going on and haven't noticed a thing either. The excitement builds up inside of me. I can already sense the other Venice, the alternate world waiting for me, just have to figure out how to get there.

As we walk, the translucent figures in the balconies and on the doorsteps as well, keep on multiplying. Some fly away, some drop in. Their laughter and mocking grow in intensity.

"The tiny little boy that walked with interlocking fingers in between his parents in Prague is back," says another dirty old transparent pirate with a black patch on one eye.

"Interlocking fingers? Are you kidding me? What a waste. There's no room for kiddies in here…Hahaha, Hahaha, Hahaha, a man that looks like a thug dressed in black clothes from another era laughs aloud at me.

I know better this time, so I ignore them.

"Let's have a seat over here," the blind old man indicates to us.

Right after we order our drinks, for me a hot chocolate, and for the adults Italian espressos, he is ready to restart.

"The San Marco clock is wicked," he announces and immediately has our undivided attention.

A fascinating silence ensues. In just a brief moment he has captured our imaginations.

"The legend is that ever since the original clock mechanism -built by Gian Paolo Rainieri and his son Giancarlo in the late 1770s- was entirely replaced in

1752 by Bartholomeous Ferracina with a new advanced design including a Graham- dead beat escapement with a 4-meter pendulum, the original builders, Gian Paolo, and Giancarlo restless spirits roam around the clock tower. It is believed that they seek revenge on the horologist Ferracina who built the new clock mechanism. And although for generations the descendants of the Rainieris inhabited the clock tower serving the city as "temperatores" (the clock keepers), that was never quite enough to put their vengeful spirits to rest. But when the temperatore's position was terminated in 1998 and the Rainieris descendants were no longer living in the tower, the belief is that as a consequence Gian Paolo's and Giancarlo's spirits have continued to roam free through its chambers, especially the one that houses The San Marco astrological clock."

Our drinks have become cold as we listen to the blind man. "As far as I can remember, there have been rumors around the city that the old-time machine comes alive at

night. It is said that even the clock's hands and the ringing-bell Shepherd-moors come alive as well. The word is that there's another Venice. A sort of alternative city," he says.

"Do you know how to gain access to it?" I ask.

"No, nobody knows. If you are so interested, that is for you to find out," he adds just before we thank him and get under way to Venice's premier Antique wizardry book's shop.

Not long after, while walking between my aunt and uncle, over Venice's narrow streets, we cross one of the city's countless small arched bridges that cross over water channels filled with gondolas and gondoliers.

The translucent figures are not only back but have multiplied in number. Some fly by, others hover right in front of me, but I ignore them.

Then the three of us see it across another small and narrow bridge. The five-story building is pastel orange in color, the name sign is painted in a rainbow of colors and is sprinkled with tiny hand-painted stars and lightning bolts.

The swoosh of air catches me by surprise. The familiar, almost imperceptible weight on my right shoulder is totally unexpected. I twist and turn to try to catch a glimpse.

"Are you alright caro (dear)?"

My aunt asks totally unaware of my visitor.

"I'm perfectly fine auntie," I reply while I try to contort more discretely.

There he is, my purported conscience, the spec of a man that the six of us harlequins referred to as Thumbpee back in Prague. As usual, he sits on my shoulder, hand on chin, with a crossed leg. His pasty white skin color and nervous energy are unchanged as he admonishes me once more.

"Erasmus, you are elate." "What do you mean late?"

"All your fellow harlequins have already made it to the other - alternate- Venice."

"Again?"

"Yes, again!"

"But how?"

"That's for you to figure out. But don' take too long, otherwise you'll be left out of this year's quest."

I stare at him with perplexed eyes. I'm lost and not even close to figuring things out.

"Trust the words of the blind man. Trust yourself and remember you are now a wizard apprentice."

Once more, before I have time to respond, he vanishes in an instant as he usually does. Still mulling about it, moments later the three of us walk into the store.

There's a strong smell of old leather and paper. On a tall-encased glass cabinet, a cape, a robe, a wand, and a coned cap are on display. The vestment set is made of a sparkling cloth of intense violet color filled with tiny yellow stars. Throughout the store the book titles include incantation formulas and conjures about how to do black magic. There are others about witches. Yet the place feels like a spiritless exhibition. Perhaps is because...the store is apparently empty. We call for help but nobody answers. Right in the center of the store, there is a small round wooden table. On it lays a massive antique book. It's wide open. The colors of the hand-painted pages jump out from afar. I approach and the writing immediately catches my attention. Almost unaware of it, I start to read aloud for the three of us.

"The Academy of the Absurdity and Ignorance"
(including the Outrageous and Ridiculous)

All appears to be normal,

as expected, and predictable.

Everything seems familiar,

known, comfy, but isn't.

The young girl's jolly strides are bouncy,
spirited, and carefree.

She arrives early,
driven by enthusiasm, desire, and curiosity.

The Academy of Absurdity and Ignorance baffles her.

Why does she have to go through this?
What do these people teach?
She asks herself drawing a blank.

"If you don't attend and complete their program,

you'll be expelled from school,"
she is told by her high school principal.

"Good morning, you must be?"

States the educational institute's host.
"An insurgent teen," replies the young girl.
"A rebel in urgent need of tutelage, I understand,"
observes the host.
"Sort of..."
Blurts inspirited the young girl.
"I gather you are not here voluntarily?"

Quizzes rhetorically the host.

"Kind of," babbles the uninterested and restless girl.
"Fair enough, follow me,"
the eccentric lady instructs.

"What do you teach here?" Asks a puzzled young girl.
"Anything that does not make sense,
we study the ridiculous,
we learn from the outrageous.
We also educate respect to ignorance

and reverence to the lack of knowledge.
We provide tutelage about
the absence of good judgment or the lack of common sense,
in other words, we teach absurdity,"
the peculiar host announces.

"Lead the way please,"
now fully interested, the restless teen says.
The young girl's full-face grimaces followed
by a wrinkled brow.
In other words, a conspicuously frowned rictus.

"Since you are a rebel,
the teachings you'll receive here
should all be Taylor-made for you.

"Why?"

"Everything taught to you in here

will be things that don't make any sense, in other words,

it'll be only about that what you love."

"But if these are all bad things,

why would anyone teach them?"

"We teach the absurd, outrageous and ridiculous

to learn the value of not being like that."

"How could I begin to comprehend such a lesson?"

"The principle behind what we teach is that we go in the

opposite direction of what is normally taught."

"I'm lost; you have to explain yourself better."

"The idea is that if you know about something in depth,

you realize its true value or absurdity,

you understand its logic or outrageousness,

you get its common sense or ridiculousness."

The young rebel girl's eyes brighten

as she finally clicks

and all the ideas about absurdity and outrageousness

inundate and finally reach her.

"If I teach you to respect ignorance

either you embrace such aberrant and mediocre behavior,

or you rebel against and end up rejecting it."

"Hence the value of studying

absurdity, outrageousness, and ridiculousness."

As I finish, just like me, my aunt and uncle are drawing blanks. A growing anxiety keeps on building inside of me. Time is ticking away and I'm still not even one inch closer to The Orloj. So, I believe.

'What does this writing have to do with my quest?' I try to reason within myself.

"It's got to be something absurd. It is that outrageous, that I've totally missed how obvious it is," now I say aloud but still talking to myself. "I need to go back to the wizardry museum, the old site of the Kraus Antique Bookstore," I say as in a crazy state.

My awesome aunt and uncle tag alone. They're happy to chaperone me in the pursuit of my fantasy. One more time we ride a gondola to our destination. Right after we enter the wizardry museum for the second time, the revelation finally gets to me.

"So, it seems absurd, but it isn't," I say aloud, "Kraus' store in Prague does exist, even though it seems absurd to believe so."

"What's the point, Erasmus?" asks my puzzled uncle Bartholomeous.

"If the Prague store exists even though it appears not to, Kraus' Venice store exists as well," I say aloud, "Trust yourself, you're now a wizard apprentice," I continue saying to myself while recalling Thumbpee's words of wisdom.

I swipe my hand across and wait but nothing happens. My aunt and uncle look bemused. I don't pay attention and walk straight out of the museum. Then, I stand in front of the faded sign" "Zbynek Kraus' Antique Bookstore for the Dark Arts and Occult Sciences."

I place my hand on it. It feels warm. "What is it?" I press myself. "Why is the sign now missing the date the store was founded?" I continue to spitfire the questions in a rant. "I need a spell. Swiping my hand is not enough!"

I slowly walk back inside the store and sit discouraged. I recall The Orloj words back at Prague's castle: "You are now wizard apprentices."

I recall how he welcomed us at the castle, and then he took us through a portal. It suddenly hits me. 'I got it!' I realize. Next, a sense of euphoria quickly engulfs me. With impetus, I stand up with my aunt and uncle following my every move. Right between the museum exhibits I swipe my hand and say the same magic

word articulated in Prague by The Orloj.

"Klementinum"

In an instant, out of the blue, the blind old man enters the store and walks towards us. As he approaches his beard fades away, followed by his glasses, hat, and clothes.

"Oh!" I exclaim, while he smiles at us, "Mr. Kraus, you were the..." I say.

"That's right, ever since you arrived in Venice, I've been close to you all along."

Both my aunt and uncle's expressions are unforgettable-surprised, in awe, and full of wonder.

"Come with me young man, it's time to go to work," he says.

Suddenly the images around me become blurry, then I see

myself contemplating my astonished aunt and uncle from a distance. They are no longer moving as if time has frozen for them. I know from my previous quest in Prague that my next 24-hours will be just a few minutes for them when I come back. They won't know the details of what I did but will have a general idea about it. As my eyes start to refocus, my aunt and uncle's images slowly fade away. Ahead of me, Mr. Kraus waves at me to continue moving. Then he's gone! I stand still as my eyesight readjusts. I'm standing over a highly elevated scaffold, inside the mechanism of a giant clock. The heart of the time exacting machine mechanism is right in front of me. With tentative steps, I walk in the direction of the back of the clock dials.

On the side of the enormous round sphere that marks the hours and minutes I see the slice of a carousel. Part of it rotates inside the clock's giant chamber. When I move in its direction, the carousel starts to move. Without thinking I hop in and ride it. The carousel's rotation takes me to the open air of the San Marco Square. However, the carousel stops after half-a- turn. From a couple of stories high I can see the full length of the beautiful square, all the way to the water's edge. It's a full moon night. Somehow time has moved forward a few hours.

Chapter 3
Meeting the Ancient Clock

"About time Blunt!"

I hear the name I used during last year's quest from underneath and seem to recognize Sang-Chang, aka Breezie's voice. As I look down, I see for the second year in a row my 5 harlequin friends leaning on each other like old pals but looking at me with impatient eyes. I glance at myself and corroborate that once more I'm wearing my blue harlequin suit.

"We're already late, use the ladder Blunt!" Firee urges me.

I slide myself down the ladder and on an instant, I join them.

"Why did it take you so long to figure it out?" Asks Sofia, aka Reddish.

"Simple, last year you all got to antiquarian Kraus after you asked around the city who was the foremost expert in wizardry in town. So, this year you all had an advantage over me, you knew that the portal was at his place. In my case, I met him in Prague as my parents had made an appointment with him as an antiquarian. So, I was not certain if the portal he opened for me was randomly located there or not. I had to find out that he was the wizardry expert on both towns."

The thunderous voice cuts across my words. "Blunt is right," the gigantic clock says.

"He had it way more difficult than any of you," The Orloj says as we all look back up to the clock's main sphere.

"But I am extremely proud how all of you, once you were on the right track, figured out the spell to make it here."

"Welcome to Venice, young harlequins. You'll have 24 hours to complete your quest and become young wizards," he says with solemnity. "This time around you are going to locate six bell-ringing Shepherd-moors. Two of them are in use at the clock's procession display. Four of them are spares. They'll be shape-shifting and adopting different personas, according to the circumstances, for example they could be street musicians or vendors, or they could be acrobats, even regular folks. Yet, remember that their preferred occupation is that of book antiquarians." The ancient watch continues, "each one of them will guide and teach you about one human virtue or vice. On this your second year, you'll have to master the virtues of Honesty, Loyalty, and Forgiveness as well as the three vices of Deceit, Betrayal, and Grudges. Each time you complete one of them, you'll earn a clue and a power," he goes on holding our total attention.

"You'll need each of the clues to be able to cross an imaginary bridge, which will be available just for you to cross to the neighboring tiny island directly in front of this square where the hollow-bay area (the basin) meets the grand canal. If you make it to the island, at the St. Giorgio Maggiore Church, you'll be given the credentials of young wizards," adds the time exacting machine. "All the powers you were granted in Prague are still with you while you are here, but I suggest that you always favor finding and learning to use your wizardry first," The Orloj continues.

"Each time you have two new clues in hand come to see me for guidance," he reminds us and continues, "as in Prague, my sons, the two clock hands will serve as your guides throughout the quest." Then, he concludes: "Finally, The Gondoliers, particularly, the one that is a mean dwarf, see these festivities, including the presence of wizards, enchanters, conjurers, witches, and magicians as a threat to their existence. They believe this menace to be bigger than the "vaporetti" (diesel powered water buses) and the motor launch taxis that have reduced their fleet from 10,000+ to just a few hundred gondolas. In particular, the gnome will be trying hard to derail or make you fail in your quest. Be aware of him at all times." The Orloj seemingly concludes but he is not ready yet. "Ah! Before I forget. As you know, I seldom move from here. Believe me, you don't want me around uninvited. Don't force me to remedy something you've done. I warn you again, when that happens, heads roll! With that being said, your 24 hours begin now," he says before silence engulfs us once again.

Venice's San Marco square seems now empty without the powerful presence of the ancient clock.

Chapter 4
The Venetian Quest Begins

The six of us meander around the square heading towards the bay. We hear a flute - a sweet and magic melody. At first sight, everything seems to be quiet, but we know better. On the sides of the San Marco Square, we see several street painters. They're scattered all around.

"Were they there a moment ago?" I ask.

The six of us look at each other. Our faces indicate that we all seem to think that the square was totally empty. As we approach, we can see views and sights of the city on their canvases. There must be 30 of them or so, spread across the big square. Some of the oil paintings depict the Grand Canal that runs across and cuts right through the heart of the city. Some of the paintings reflect the moonlight reflected on the Canal, creating a special silver lining effect refracting and illuminating the citadel's architecture on the water. Most of the paintings though, show the golden colors of "The Basilica" (The Cathedral) of San Marco, the pink hues of the Square's "Palazzo" (Palace), and the red- brick towers of "Di Campanile" (Landlord) as the tower of the square was called in the old times. The colors all around are bright and shiny. The backgrounds are the same narrow alleyways and streets, bridges, water canals, gondolas, and especially the palaces. But the subjects are all different. Soon we are all transfixed by one particular painting. It's huge, perhaps 15x30 feet. It has multiple scenes of the island city organized in a circle, like a carousel, around a central huge image.

"It's like a Venetian mosaic," I say.

"Certo (right) ragazzi (youngster), certo," says the painter. We are all mesmerized by the masterpiece. "Young harlequins, I gather," The painter says.

"We all know who you are," is the strident voice we suddenly hear.

We turn around and see a painter sitting on a highchair. He has a really ugly nose. It's corrugated, long, pointy, and thick. He's slightly hunched, and his voice is high-pitched; his hair is red and spiky. His eyes are incessantly moving and downright scary, their look is simply devilish… At that point, I see his short legs. 'He's a gnome,' I think while remembering The Orloj's cautionary words. I know every one of my fellow Harlequins is listening to my thoughts.

"Do you want to take a look at my works? Come on follow me, they're all stored at my place nearby," he says as he jumps to the floor.

"Your canvas is empty," Firee points out.

"Well, I was just about to get started," he says defensively.

"In that case, we'll come back later to admire your work," says Greenie as we all turn around and focus on the Venetian mosaic.

At that moment, the obfuscated gnome simply disappears in a cloud of dust.

"The gnome is gone!" Points a relieved Checkered.

"For the moment Reddish. I'm sure we'll see more of him later on and it won't be this nice. Now he's really mad," I point out.

"That was a very wise decision, the one you just made," says the painter of the Venetian mosaic who is still busy at work.

"Tell us about all the different images of Venice you're painting," says Checkered.

He has penetrating green eyes and his clothes are all stained with paint. We're all mesmerized as we contemplate his painting.

"Venice is not an island," he continues now with a flow of words we don't quite follow. With our faces wearing interrogation marks, he continues…

"Venice is actually a mosaic of 118 islands, separated by 180 Canals 28 miles in length. They're all connected by a network of 400 small bridges that are the extensions of 90 miles of narrow streets. There are hundreds of palaces and countless Churches here. Most of them hold timeless treasures along with dark secrets and cryptic mysteries. The canvas of our magnificent city you've named - a Venetian Mosaic- is waiting for you all. However, first and foremost, you must go to the "Ponte Dei Sospiri (The Bridge of Sighs)," he says as he continues to paint.

We shrug our shoulders and continue to walk. Reddish breaks rank and walks back with a curious face. She wants to take a second look at several of the small paintings within the mosaic's carousel. We observe her puzzled. She suddenly shakes her head and returns to us.

"Guys," she announces in a loud voice trying to get our attention towards the magnetic painting. "There's something in that painting that does not make sense just like in most of the paintings in here," she says referring to the scattered painters throughout the square.

Firee's eyes illuminate. "That's right, it is nighttime here," he says, "Except for a few, all these paintings reflect broad daylight." Reddish says, "Why would anyone paint day images at night, without the benefit of the light colors?"

"It's absurd, isn't it?" I blurt out, but as I complete the question, I recall the Academy of the Absurd and Ridiculous reading earlier in the day.

"That's precisely what it is," says the voice of my conscience. Thumbpee is back on my shoulder, hand on chin, with one crossed leg. I twist and turn trying to get a glimpse of the minuscule man. It's only through an extreme contortion of my neck that I do.

"Do we have anything to find in regard to the absurdity of those paintings at this time of the night?" I ask Thumbpee.

"You all are now wizard apprentices. It's up to you to take actions as such. Besides, this second time around you have to figure things out, all by yourselves," he says. Before I can react, Thumbpee vanishes in an instant once more.

Out of instinct, following her gut, Greenie takes a step forward and impulsively lifts her right arm and draws a circle with her right palm in front of the painting. The carousel of images rotates following the same exact pace of her circling hand. When she stops, the images' rotation also stops. The central grand image changes at the same pace as the rotating images.

"The larger image is a blowout of the smaller ones whenever each reaches the top of the carousel," Breezie says.

We all focus and catch up immediately with his opportune realization.

"A magic oil painting?" Greenie asks rhetorically.

The frantic buzz of Buggie's flapping wings catches all by surprise. The flying bug hovers around us, drawing circles frantically. Then, his tiny green laser points to the image of a covered narrow bridge. Buggie then points his tiny laser beam towards me. This followed by him pointing to the same small image again. The flying bug continues to do the same as I move the carousel by drawing a circle. I do not stop until the desired image reaches the slot at the top. Now we see the blowout image of the covered small bridge in the center of the painting. At first no one knows what to do.

"That must be the bridge of sighs," Reddish says.

"First and foremost, we have to go there," Greenie says.

"We have to learn to help ourselves with wizardry, when necessary," I recall aloud.

Instinctively, I follow Buggie's command, and without thinking, expecting to ridicule myself, I repeat the same spell I used earlier, "Klementinum," I say aloud.

That's when the central image becomes blurry. Suddenly, right in front of us, a portal emerges. Acting on impulse, I simply hop into the portal. Almost in an instant, I land on the actual bridge of sighs. My fellow five harlequins follow right after me. We turn around and see the blurry rectangular image of the portal on the painting.

"Guys, remember this location. This is the exact portal location to go back."

"Close!" Intuitively I command and the portal closes.

It's all new to us, but we are quickly learning to be wizards.

"Guys! We barely moved, look," says Greenie.
We all turn around and see through the night, the silhouettes, and shadows of the back of the buildings of the San Marco Square. Protuberating on top of them, the San Marco Basilica and the Campanile tower can be seen as well.

"There must be a purpose for us to come here through a portal and now be standing in this bridge just a few hundred yards always from our starting point," Breezie says.

"You're absolutely right," are the words of my conscience. Thumbpee is back on my shoulder!

"You are standing in what is perhaps the most famous bridge in all of Venice. It connects from the back of the San Marco square -that you are staring at now- to the Palazzo Ducale (The Doge's Palace) with the site of old Venice Republic's Prison. Way before the bridge was built all sorts of atrocities were committed on this site. This bridge symbolizes the romantic tale of how the suffering ended. Harlequins, you need to figure out how that legend relates to the virtues or vices you have to find. You can rest assured that one of the bell-ringing Shepherd Moors lie close by in waiting," explains Thumbpee in his longest talk since we met him. Intent on asking, I react quickly.

"Thumb..." to no avail. He's already gone.

"Where to go first?" Asks Checkered.

"We go against our instincts and do something absurd," grudgingly I say, still getting acquainted with the use of absurdity and outrageousness.

Everyone nods or consents in their own peculiar way. With trepidation, we walk off the bridge towards the old Venice republic prison site. As we approach another portal - seemingly a blurry door appears in front of us. Without stopping we cross it. In front of us lies a compact building with the shape of a castle. It is dark in color and the absence of any windows is intimidating.

"Sinister," Reddish says. None of us say a word.

"The whole thing is translucent," Firee says, as we are all mesmerized by the transparent glow of the old prison.

As I am about to take a step forward, Breezie grabs my arm.

"Blunt, look down!" He says.

In front of us, there is another canal. It seems to go around the prison. It is sprinkled with silver and whites' reflections of the full moon.

"That wasn't there a moment ago," I exclaim with my heart racing.

That's when we hear the tremendous chirring noise of a couple of enormous chains rolling down on each of its sides. An enormous wooden door is lowered down until it lands softly on the ground acting as a bridge over the small channel. We all contemplate in eerie silence the entrance of the ghostly place. An owl announces itself in the still of the night, adding creepiness to the situation.

"I'm not going in there," Greenie says with a shaky voice.

Before she's done though, I'm already moving forward so there's not much time for any of us to process her words.

We stand in an open yard surrounded by the menacing tall walls of the place. Behind our backs, we hear the sound of the two gigantic chains pulling the bridge back up until the entrance is once more shut. This time with all of us inside.

Coming out of nowhere, the giant moor stands in front of us. His dark skin blends with the night shades. He wears the armored suit of a gladiator with only his chest and head protected and his muscular extremities exposed.

"Follow me harlequins,"

Sheepishly, we obediently walk behind him as he unlocks thick and heavy metal doors, one after another, for us to step in and then locks them again as we enter each chamber. We continue to move forward and start to descend floor after floor, immersing ourselves deeper and deeper into the old prison.

When we finally reach the cell rows, ghostly skeletal faces peek out between the bars of each small cell window. We hear the pleads and short phrases filled with pain and anguish. Their sounds deafen our reluctant steps over the wet stone floors. Finally, we reach a humid and dark chamber. It has a three-story high ceiling. All the instruments and artifacts we see are downright scary: The wooden wheel to stretch, the benches with holes to lock head and arms, the hanging chains, the whips. It's a torture chamber!

"Have a seat," the giant moor guard says.

There are no seats except for the torture benches. We hesitate.

"I said. Have a seat!" He commands, this time we comply.

Then without further communication, he exits with pompous long steps.

"What are we doing here?" Asks Checkered.

"We have to figure it out," I say aloud.

At first, we only see a fast-moving shadow. When a clearer image comes into view, we realize that is the gnome walking towards us with short bouncy steps. His long, pointy, corrugated nose and his tiny eyes darting back and forth are his two most distinctive features.

"What do we have here? Of course, the six wizard apprentices," he says with a high-pitched and strident voice.

We look at each other in disbelief but otherwise say nothing. As we can read each other's thoughts, I do remind everyone of the warning we received earlier about avoiding the dwarf at all costs during our quest.

"Somehow you all disappeared on me at the square. I'm only trying to help you."

"You mean with trapping nets?" I ask.

"That's only for your protection," falsely he says.

And you want us to believe that?" Reddish asks

"Please accept my apologies," he says avoiding eye contact.

We all stare at him with deeply skeptical eyes.

"Tell you what. I imagine that all of you want to get out of this place, right?" He asks.

"Yes!" Blurts out Breezie then sees in our faces that we're not pleased with his impulsivity.

"I could help you break out of here if you want me to?"

This time none of us says a word. We can see the gnome's face turning red in an instant.

"You don't want my help, FINE!" He says swiping his hand, "let's see how you get out this one all by yourselves," the furious dwarf says walking away. As he disappears in the darkness of the torture chamber, he swipes his hand again as if casting a conjure. In an instant we're caged in a cube of translucent steel bars. A massive jail cell on top and around us -right where we are sitting. In the background, we can hear the dwarf's sarcastic laughter. Then the steel bars of our cell start to close on us and with it, our sudden place of imprisonment becomes smaller by the minute.

"Well, we know none of this is real," reflects Breezie aloud.

"It sure feels real to me," says Greenie.

"We are inside of a prison, what do you expect otherwise?" says Firee.

"But are we?" I ask.

"What's your point Blunt?" Asks an impatient Breezie.

"That perhaps we aren't," I reply.

"Now you totally lost me," Breezie says.

"You lost us all, Blunt," adds Reddish.

"Maybe the jail is only in our minds," I add. Everyone is paying close attention now.

"We know the place doesn't exist since centuries ago and yet we all feel like it does. But this is only our imagination at work. Let us all think about the empty plot of land we saw from the bridge of sighs. Let's picture it in our minds. Feel the light breeze whistling over it and the leaves being lifted from the vacant ground. Listen to the lone owl in the night," I plead to all. One by one I stare at my fellow harlequins with convincing eyes.

"Close your eyes and feel it," I say as I do it myself.

A short while later, suddenly I feel the light breeze and hear the noctambulant owl. I open my eyes at the same time as the other 5 do as well; we are all standing in the middle of the empty lot, the bridge of sighs just a few hundred yards away. The diminutive voice of my conscience comes straight into my ear, "well done harlequins. In life is easy to get trapped in our own mental prisons. Many people are trapped in their own internal jails. All of it resides in their own imagination. They don't really exist but inside of their own minds," Thumbpee says while sitting on my shoulder; hand on his chin and one leg crossed on top of the other. Then in a fraction of a second, before I can react, he vanishes once again.

Suddenly the owl's cryptic chant is replaced by the annoying buzz of Buggie incessantly flapping his tiny wings. To catch our attention the buzz pitch intensifies. We turn around and see his tiny green laser beam pointing to the small, covered bridge of sighs then to the back of the Doge's Palace. Promptly we follow and walk over the bridge and around the back of the palace, next, we enter San Marco's square.

"Wait a minute guys, we've just made a serious mistake," says Greenie.

At first, we look clueless, but it doesn't take long for all of us to realize what is it that we missed. We turn back walk to the bridge and this time is Checkered who says the magic word at the exact spot. "Klementinum!" she says, and the blurry portal door reappears. We all step into it and right away are standing back at the San Marco square in front of the Palazzo Ducale (The Doge's Palace) with its pink marble facade and its lions, 75 of them. I recall what my uncle Roberto had said earlier in the day, "The Lion is the symbol of Venice. It protects Venice and makes the city safe. That's why they call it "La Serenissima" (the calmest of all cities). The Palace's main massive entrance doors are slightly ajar as we step inside and through its gothic arches. Buggie's buzz increases frantically, his tiny green laser bean points to a massive golden set of stairs. The ornate interiors of the palace are rich in color and eye-catching in size. Upstairs the chambers are each more exquisitely decorated than the other with enormous renaissance doors. One particular chamber is lighted more intensely than the others. We enter with curiosity; 4 massive paintings cover the high ceiling room. The moment we are all in, the door behind us closes up. We scramble to try to open it, then try 3 other doors in the chamber but they are locked, the entire chamber is shut down. With no place to sit, we remain standing for a few seconds.

"Why don't we pull the ornament ropes hanging next to the paintings," Wonders Firee as we contemplate the 8 of them, 2 per painting.

I try a couple, but nothing happens. Then Checkered pulls another one and instantaneously the enormous painting rolls up uncovering the glass window display of an antique Bookstore. It is a shop we are already familiar with.

"Antique Books for the Spirit and Soul,"
(est. long, long time ago).

"The last time we were at this place was atop a cathedral in Prague," reminds us Greenie.

We walk in and to our surprise, the interior is exactly the same as the first time. Cylindrical in shape and impossibly high bookshelves. Right at the center of the store, we see a familiar face dear to all of us, that of one Cornelious Tetragor, the antiquarian with a massively long white beard; he's wearing a matching long white robe. He is already waiting for us.

"Welcome, welcome to Venice, youngsters."

"I gather your antique bookstore travels with you, Sir." I say in jest.

"Indeed, it does. As a matter of fact, no matter what I do; my old, trusted tower is always just one spell away," he says with a benign smile.

"Mr. Tetragor our quest has covered very little terrain, Sir," Firee says.

"How so?"

"Right outside of this palace at San Marco Square, we all jumped into a portal on a magic painting, just to turn out a few hundred yards away on the bridge of sighs at the back of this palace, then after a peculiar visit to The Republic of Venice old Prison, we crossed the portal back and it took us to the entrance of the palace where your store currently is," adds Fire

"Sometimes in life, we have to travel long distances to accomplish very little. On other occasions, our journeys are short, but our results are huge."

Mr. Tetragor contemplates each one of us as if scrutinizing all our reactions.

"Besides, there are moments when you don't know how to get somewhere. Needing a bit of help, you take it, and voila, you are there!" He adds, "I also watched your visit to the old-republic prison. Tell me, what did you learn from your experience over there?" Mr. Tetragor asks.

"It was a scary place, Sir. We realized that it didn't really exist but only within our imagination," Reddish says.

"That's right, dear. We build walls inside ourselves. We become our own obstacle. Many of us live inside an internal prison, hence we don't feel free. All we have to do is open our eyes and see reality," Mr. Tetragor says.

Without another word the old antiquarian walks always and deftly starts to climb one of his impossible high ladders. Up he goes the bookshelves that plaster his circular store. He must be 60 to 90 feet high up the ladder when stops. A small dot is how he looks. He pulls a book and drops it in a sac hanging from his shoulder, then he slides down at full speed with his hands and feet on the sides of the ladder. Just short of the ground, he slows down and hops to the ground. We are all in awe, mouths open, and happy to see him perform his amazing feat for the second time.

"Harlequins, I have here a reading that will illustrate well a virtue you always have to treasure, practice, and maintain in life.

"The Young Shepherd and the Tarot Reader"

Early on a Sunday morning, her only free day of the week.
The Young Girl pedals down
The Arlberg mountains sinuous road.
She is coming down to visit the traveling-gypsy's caravan.

Ever since she can remember
she's been a Sheep Shepherd
as her father, grandfather,
and every other family-head ancestors were back in time.
All of them male but her though,
The Young Shepherd has broken
a deeply rooted tradition of the Austrian Alps.

At an early age her inclination and passion
for her father's job
had slowly persuaded him that his rightful heir
was his precious daughter.

The gypsies' convoy is parked just outside the alpine village.
From afar she can see the vivid colors
Of the visiting performers' wagons, tents, and clothes.
Some of the gypsies are dancing, others juggling,
one is on a one-wheel cycle, another acrobatic pirouettes.

A small crowd is gathered around each act.
The patrons applaud and cheer.
They reward the act with coins and bills,
dropping them on the customary hats
lying on the floor next to each set of performers.

The Tarot reader's wagon has a long line waiting,
the Young Shepherd drops her bike a joins the queue.

Time flies by as she watches
the spectacle of street performers.
When her turn finally arrives,
she is eager and ready.

With trepidation,
she climbs the three steps old train wagon,
hesitantly opens the cracking door,
and slowly enters the mysterious place.

The incense smell is strong, sweet, and inundates her.
As her eyes adjust to the darkness of the room
she sees her standing with greeting arms and a smile.

The Tarot reader is a mane of curly dark hair
cascading over her round face.
She has piercing eyes and thick eyebrows.
She wears a loose colorful dress,
it reaches her ankles and wrists.
She has a pair of gigantic rings hanging from her ears.
A crystal ball filled with smoke
sits on a small table next to the Tarot Reader.

What do we have here?
A beautiful young girl from the mountains?"
The young Shepherd nods in confirmation.
Gently the Tarot reader picks up
the young Shepherd's hands.
"Ah, I see, but you are not a common girl,"
the Tarot Reader says,
"come dear, have a seat."
She leads the young woman to the small table,
and they sit facing each other.

The crystal ball sitting on the side table, becomes active.
Gases expand and begin to move within,
shades and color tones spread through it.

"Tell me dear, what do you want to know today?"

"What does the future hold for me?"
"For you, the future holds anything you may desire."
"For me. How come? Why?"
"You're special." "Do you tell this to everyone?"

The Tarot Reader smiles but her eyes denote surprise.

"Not quite, Dear, not quite." She says.

"Tell me, beautiful girl,
what troubles you about the future?"

"I'm a Shepherd and a good one indeed."
"Not only wonderful but a noble profession as well."
"There aren't many women Shepherds either."
"Are there any at all?" Asks the Tarot Reader.
"I've been told there are a few
but I have yet to meet one."

"There you go dear, you're special."
"Well, I wonder if I could be something else."
"Why would you wish to be so?"
"Sometimes I dream if I could be a writer or perhaps a painter?"
"In life, we can be anything we set our hearts into."
"Will I?"
The young Shepherd girl implies staring at the crystal ball.

"Let's take a look," the Tarot Reader says.

"Dear, sometimes our desire to do or be something else
is an excuse to escape from the truth.
Gently the Tarot Reader takes the Shepherd's hands
and places them on top of the crystal ball.

An image of the Alpine country appears on the crystal ball.

"Who's that?" Asks the Tarot Reader.
The young Shepherd girl's mouth is fully open.
Her face denotes total surprise.

"That's my brother."

The Tarot reader rotates her hand around the crystal ball.
The image repeats herself several times
at different times and days.

"He has a guilty look," points out the Tarot Reader.
The young Shepherd girl watches the images mesmerized.
"Is he stealing sheep from the herd?"
The young Shepherd nods.

A couple of tears slowly slide down her cheeks.

The Tarot reader moves her hands over the crystal ball again,
the images scroll by showing
the young Shepherd's brother selling the sheep in town.
Next, he can be seen on multiple occasions
sitting in a room full of smoke and liquor.

"He's a gambler," The Tarot Reader says.
The young Shepherd woman cries and sobs.

The Tarot Reader once again
covers the crystal ball with her hands.
It now shows the image of an old man admonishing
-in several instances- the young Shepherd woman.
"That's your father and you've taken the blame for your brother
on the missing sheep."

The young Shepherd now cries inconsolably.

The Tarot Reader stands and embraces her.
"This is the reason you want to know about your future?"
The Tarot Reader whispers with a loving tone.

"This is why you wonder if you could be something else?"
She adds with tender care in her words.

For the first time the young Shepherd
lifts her teary eyes and looks at the Tarot Reader
straight in the eyes and nods.
"Well, you've come to the right place my girl,"
she leans back facing the young Shepherd.

She then takes both her hands again.

"Honesty begins within," she says cryptically.

The young Shepherd girl's eyes grow wide then glow as she
begins to understand.
"We have first to be honest with ourselves
before we preach or profess honesty to others."

The Tarot reader now has
the young Shepherd's undivided attention.
"You love what you do right?"
"Yes!"

"A Shepherd is what you were born to be. Isn't it right?"
"Absolutely true."
"It's what you've been since an early age."
Shyly the young girl nods.
"There's dignity in every legitimate job or profession.

There's no valid reason for you
to abandon what you love, except dishonesty.
You feel ashamed for your sibling's actions,
yet you are not truthful with yourself about his bad deeds,
you haven't been able to confront him.

Instead, you've been taking the blame for him.
Not being honest with yourself,
has led you to not being honest
with either your brother or your father,
hence perpetuating dishonesty within your family.

Your father is upset at you wrongly believing you are at fault,
your brother neither respects nor fears you,
so, he continues to steal sheep from your herd.

Now, to top it all
you want to quit and bolt out of the situation,
thinking that is the solution."

"What do you suggest I do then?"
"First and foremost be honest with yourself.
Ask yourself, what is the truth?
Spell it out to yourself first.
Then go and confront your sibling,
Demand that he goes and takes full responsibility
in front of your father.
If he doesn't, go ahead and do it yourself.
Also, demand that he pays back the sheep he stole.
After all, they don't belong to either of you,
they belong to your parents.

Once you do this,
you'll begin to enjoy being a Shepherd again."

Cornelious Tetragor looks solemn and circumspect as he finishes reading.

"Harlequins, what have you learned from this reading?"

"In order to be honest, I must be honest with myself first," says Checkered.

"Honesty begins within me," says Breezie.

"Exactly, honesty is a virtue we project on ourselves first before we can project it on others," says the wise antiquarian.

"There's another important lesson. What is it?" He asks.

"The lack of honesty with ourselves spreads throughout all our actions affecting our lives the lives of others," says Firee.

"Excellent! Bravo. Here you go, harlequins you've now mastered the virtue of honesty," Mr. Tetragor says handing Firee a white envelope labeled "Honesty."

We all smile in celebration while Mr. Tetragor in one sweep move snaps his fingers and just like that, we are back right to out starting point, right in the middle of the San Marco Square, and under a cloudless -full moon- night sky.

"Remember, it works better when you open them in pairs," says Thumbpee, suddenly back in my shoulder.

"Thumbpee, what is our new power?" Asks Greenie.

"You've already discovered it and put it to good use," the diminutive man replies.

We all look at him -in my case I do it contorting my neck- with puzzled looks.

"You now have the ability to see reality while in the presence and surrounded by fantasy. Thus, you won't be fooled easily by it," the spec of a man says reminding us about the feat we pulled at the old republic prison translucent cell.

"Stick to the path," cryptically he adds, and once more before we can say another word he is gone!

Chapter 5
A Feast in the House of Levi

We are left standing on the empty square. The wicked sounds of the night are coming from everywhere. Laughter, swearing, swooshes of air, small explosions…
Puff... Puff…followed by stardust sprinkling and sparkling in the air. At the square's bay front, we see again the gathering of painters. Right at their sight, we know exactly where to go. "Stick to the path," repeating Thumbpee's words I say aloud
as we start to walk in their direction.

Sure enough, moments later, we are once again standing in front of the massive painting we have called "Venetian Mosaic" a kind of "painting of paintings." We face the carousel of images, and focus on the large one at the center, matching the small image at the top of the carousel. For the second time in a row, it's Greenie that takes the initiative. Lifting her right hand, she draws a circle, and the carousel rotates until it stops on an image of what appears to be a compound of unpretentious buildings.

"That group of buildings is called the "Academia." It serves as Venice's main museum and holds art masterpieces from many of Venice's most famous artists. It used to be a convent, a church, and a -scuola- (school) called -Santa Maria Della Carita- (The charitable St. Mary)," says Thumbpee reappearing and vanishing from my shoulder in a fraction of a second. In his absence, we now see the blurry image of a portal positioned right in front of the painting's central image.

"Let's go," I say before we jump one after another into the image's portal.

The Academia Museum Hall we're in is imposing. The gilded, colorful, and magnificently decorated exhibit room is full of paintings. We stroll surrounded by enormous paintings with vivid and bright colors. We see plaques with names like Veneziano, Bellini, Carpaccio, Conegliano, Tiziano, Lotto, Tiepolo, Piazzeta, Carpiera, Canaletto, Guardi…all among the greatest Venetian painters of all time.

Suddenly, Buggie's annoying buzz breaks the silence. The flying bug hovers in front of the entrance a large hall ahead of us. Curious we all walk in his direction. His tiny green laser beam is pointing at a huge painting, the plaque on the wall reads:

"Feast in the House of Levi" by Paolo Veronese.

This time is Reddish who approaches the magnificent artwork. She raises her hand -seemingly ready to touch it-

"Guys, close your eyes and imagine yourselves, as per the images on the painting, feasting at the House of Levi."

I stare at the festive image contained in the painting; next I close my eyes and imagine myself being part of it. I hope the others are doing the same. The first thing I hear is loud, non-stop laughter. Timidly, I open my eyes and find myself in the middle of a rowdy family reunion; the dishes are appealing and colorful. The servings are huge, the culinary scents and aromas are both intense and irresistible. The friendly crowd expressions are filled with joy, including the usual roasting and the storytellers. Yet, above all there's noise, it is loud and even strident; the laughter is shouted and impregnates the air with ebullient human energy and loving interactions. The six of us contemplate in awe the mélange of many. None of us know exactly what to do next.

"Visitors?" says a heavy-set lady while munching with gusto a humungous leg of lamb.

"They are dressed like court buffoons," says another spirited lady with round edges all around.

"Totally ridiculous attires, but that's the way they dress the wizard apprentices nowadays," says a distinguished and vast man in between bites, "what do you want?" suddenly he says.

Absolutely startled we don't know how to respond.

"Better said, what do you need?" He presses between munches.

"We are trying to locate an antiquarian," I say. "You mean one the clock moors?"

"Yes," I say hesitatingly.

"Well, let's begin by you joining us. We shall eat first, shall we? Then we can talk. Perhaps we may be able to help you."

The six of us feast like hungry tigers. The noisy clan leaves no room for any of us to participate but they accept our presence, so we're happy just to listen and observe the eccentricities flying all around us.

In the end, we are not just satiated; we're filled up to capacity. We are also entertained and relaxed. It should be said though that although it all sounds and looks like a normal family reunion, the occurrence is anything but that. To begin with, the "Levi clan" is all translucent as in we see right through each one of them. Then there is the levitation stuff. Gravity is absent altogether. The ghostly figures, food, and stuff all float. So, it is not, "pass me the sauce," instead it is simply "hover it to me, please," when anyone wants anything not yet on the table, the clan members snap their fingers and voila! It appears in an instant. Even removal of anything or anyone for inappropriate behavior is just one snap of the fingers away. The head of the clan -Mr. Levi- simply waves any of his fatty hands and the transgressor or the item not needed simply vanish in an instant. Same for scattered items, they are neatly organized right after his handsy commands. The six of us are nodding off when the patriarch of the Levi clan once more places his attention on us.

"The tall, old man with the bent hat was here earlier," he says.

We all shake off our fullness and understand immediately who he is speaking about.

"Lazarus Zeetrikus, that rascal of a man entertained us with his magic for quite a while, then left in a hurry as if possessed by the wind," the head of the Levi clan continues.

"We first met him on a tavern in Prague. As you, the crowd at that place was celebrating and feasting with great intent. But on that occasion, we caught a glimpse of him before he split, so somehow, we were able to follow him through the Czech capital labyrinthic city streets," full of exuberance Reddish says to the amused Mr. Levi.

"Well on this occasion, as wizard apprentices, you're going to have to do a lot more. All I can tell you is in which direction he's headed: When you exit, cross the small bridge in front of our home, go over the channel and turn right. 100 meters further you'll see a group of "Gondolieri" (Gondoliers). Make sure you hire the one wearing the red-white striped shirt and a black beret. Ask him to take you to Zeetrikus' place. Only he knows where old Lazarus is located.

"Aren't all gondolieri always dressed in those colors?" Asks Breezie.

"Not in the alternate version of Venice guys," the host of the feasting family says.

We walk out of the Levi family mansion (a former palace, Venetian style). We follow the directions given. While crossing the indicated small arched bridge we can already see -on the other side- a small group of gondolieri, docked on the water channel.

"Signore (Mr.) Levi was right! Look there's only one gondolieri dressed in a red and white striped shirt," says Greenie.

As we approach the docking area, there are a dozen or so gondolieri dressed in all kinds of colors.

"Guys, it can't be that easy..." Breezie interrupts himself as he realizes -and we all do as well- who the gondolieri is. It is the gnome again!

"Harlequins, this time you have no choice. I'm the only one who can take you to see Lazarus Zeetrikus," The dwarf says, and judging by what we can see, it seems to be true.

In response, the 6 of us start communicating through thoughts.

'We're facing another absurd situation,' Firee says.

'That's right. Let's think about it carefully. What about if we concentrate and try to see these groups for what they really are instead of what they appear to be," continues Firee.

"What about if we focus on discerning what each one of them is thinking?" I say referring to one of the powers we earned in Prague.

As we do this, we quickly see that in reality, all gondolieri have striped shirts except the dwarf who's dressed in black from head to toe. Among the gondolieri we quickly identify the only gondolieri wearing a red and white shirt.

'I hope the harlequins are not fooled by the ruthless dwarf. I wish I could warn them, but I'm not allowed,' we hear our gondolieri thinking, further validating our presumption.

"Well, harlequins, what are you waiting for? I don't have a lot of patience," the gnome says just before he's left speechless as we board a different gondola and immediately get underway.

"Dwarf, we know you altered our perception of reality. But it failed. We didn't fall for it," Breezie says.

Once more the gnome curses, twists, and turns in anger.

"Rest assured harlequins, I'll get you, sooner or later I'll get you. You're only making it worst for yourselves," he says just before disappearing into thin air after a small but scary explosion.

"Well done harlequins," says the gondolieri as he paddles through the city water channels. We navigate in front of countless magnificent buildings. As if reading our minds he says, "There are approximately 450 palaces and historical houses in Venice. Today they're being used as museums, stores, government, etc. None of them are damp-proof as their foundations of rough stone blocks that were built only for four feet above the water level," he explains.

Half an hour later we see a fully lit pastel peach color palazzo (palace). As we inch closer to it, the familiar store sign comes into view.

"The Jester, Antique Books for all Ages"
(Est. long, long time ago).

"Welcome to your destination," can be heard from the back, but our gondolieri has morphed into a tall man wearing a bent top-hat.

"Mr. Zeetrikus!" I blurt.

With a benevolent smile he adds, your powers don't work on the six antiquarians guiding you," he reminds us, "That's why you only saw and heard me when I wanted you to," The antiquarian says.

We all contemplate the wise antiquarian in awe and wonder while he leads us into his store.

Zeetrikus' store has a strong smell of old leather and paper. Piles upon piles of books are everywhere. The place looks messy and unkempt.

"Harlequins, I have here the perfect book for you to learn about the human flaw of holding grudges," Zeetrikus says, and he opens the book and starts to read in earnest…

"The Young Seamstress and the Jolly looking Man"

The young seamstress endlessly spins the wheel,
incessantly driving the spindle,
weaving cotton and wool threads
of all kinds, thicknesses, and colors.

Sofia labors incessantly day and night.
The young seamstress seeks perfection,
her artful creations are sought by many.
Whether dresses, cashmeres, cardigans, or scarves,
the prodigious seamstress' artisan creations,
command a premium and a long wait.

Her prowess is best appreciated
by her deftly crochet needlework,
done by her at vertiginous speed with a single thread,
and a pair of long hooked needles.

Yet with all her success,
the talented handcrafter obsesses about the past, she is
resentful of all of those,
that at the beginning of her career as seamstress, didn't believe
in her talents and chosen profession
nor did they provide support when she needed it the most.

One of the unintended consequences of her painful experiences
is that anything Sofia obsesses about.
It obfuscates her to no end.

Wisely on those moments
the young seamstress always takes a break,
and heads for a stroll
on the deep green woods
located right off the back of her workshop.

Soon she wanders through the lush nature
trying to take her mind off her grudges.

The sound of the harmonica spreads through the entire forest,
it's a soft rhythmic melody,
the faint tune is enchanting,
its precious notes soothe her.
Driven by an irresistible magnetic pull
Sofia steps softly over the pine needles.

She doesn't want to disturb the calming effect
the melody has on her.
Following the source of the comforting tune
the young seamstress inches closer and closer
-her anger and angst mitigated-
cautiously she peeks from the sides
of the trunks of the wide-tall trees.

Finally, she sees him sitting on a fallen tree.
He's a jolly-looking man
with a pleasant expression of happiness
plastered all over
his round, rosy and chubby cheeks.

The jolly-looking man
plays the harmonica with ease,
all his movements are soft and paused.
His delight is palpable.
He's transfixed seemingly basking in joy.
His eyes are closed, His eyelids relaxed.
Even his breathing is relaxed,
as if assuaged by his own melody.

Totally comfortable
he barely blows or inhales into the instrument.
"Have a seat young lady,"
the jolly-looking man says
pointing at a grassy clearing in front of him.

Still, without opening his eyes he continues to play,
Sofia hesitates at first but cautiously does as told.
"Are you enjoying the forest?"
"Kind of..."
"Why a half-hearted answer?"

Sofia is startled,
the jolly-looking man has stopped playing,
yet the music tune continues.
"A few things that bother me about the past,"
pensive she replies.
"Are you referring to matters that no longer exist?"
"Yes," she says defensively.
Bothered, she asks,
"excuse me, why do you keep your eyes closed...oh...are you?
"Blind, yes I am, but only through my eyes."
Embarrassed, Sofia struggles with what to do or say next.
"Are those memories poisoned with anger and resentment?"
The jolly-looking man asks.

"Yes."
"So, you are using and wasting your valuable time
on planet earth on the negative side of your past?"
Sofia nods in confirmation.
"Well, grudges are thieves." "Thieves?"
"Yes! They happily steal life's time from you." "Happily?"
"Oh yes. Happily, because you let them do so.
In fact, you place and keep them inside of you.
So, you are their host.
And a very good one indeed.
Naturally, your grudges don't want to leave you.
They know they are welcomed guests
within your tortured mind and spirit."

"Well jolly-looking man, fact is, they control me
I can't get rid of them!" She says protesting. "Let's face it Sofia,
it is you who doesn't want to get rid of them." "No, that's not
true...wait a minute,
how do you know my name?"

"Young Seamstress, I told you already,
I see and sense people and things
without the use or need of my eyesight."
The young seamstress' attention level raises even more.
"The first thing you need to understand
is that whatever affected you in the past
way back then, no longer exists.
It only resides in your mind and imagination,"
the jolly-looking man says.

"I think about what I resent all the time,"
"That's another reason holding grudges
is a foolish game, how senseless is to repeat
the same movie over and over again in your mind.
Besides, think about this:
Grudging makes you think or wish ill for others
but the one poisoned with anger is you."
"How do I uninvite this pack of thieves?"
"Beginning by being happy,
valuing and appreciating who you are,
what you have, whatever that is, but never, ever,
who you are not, or don't have,
much less with what you pretend to be.

Many times, we are angry at others because deep inside
we see or perceive them as better than us."
"At present, I don't do either of those two things that well."
"Finally, stop judging others
and use that energy and time to judge yourself first.
That way you constantly keep an eye on your life and actions,
propitiating growth and change within you."

"Thank you very much, jolly-looking man.
This is a life lesson that I'll treasure forever," Sofia says.

The Seamstress waving good-bye
strolls back through the forest humming along
with the same melody that continues to spread all around her.

The jolly-looking man continues to play incessantly.
On the other hand, the young seamstress laughs in joy,
finally freed from grudges -those poisonous thieves- forever.

Lazarus Zeetrikus the antiquarian with the long white beard and robe contemplates each one of us with inquisitive eyes.

"Tell me young harlequins, what have you learned Today from this fable?"

The five of us have much to ponder. In some form or another, every aspect of the moral tale alludes to and touches each one of us.

"Being resentful is an excuse," Interjects Reddish.

"Interesting...But an excuse to what?" Zeetrikus asks.

"It's the false reason we give ourselves not to confront pain or those that we believe have hurt us. It's how we fool ourselves with the excuse that we cannot forget or let go of the feelings of hurt, anger, and revenge against that or those that we avoid facing," says Greenie.

"Right...But why is that an excuse?" Zeetrikus says

"Because we let those awful-angry feelings -the so-called thieves- remain and linger unresolved in our minds and spirits. They're poisonous because we do not work -sometimes not even try- to get rid of them, - says Checkered.

"It's understandable that when something or someone hurts you, we may resent it at first. Our anger becomes an excuse when we don't let it go or we don't deal with it. The grudge is born, grows, and remains only because we let it be. No one else is responsible for the existence of a grudge but us," Firee adds.

A pensive Lazarus Zeetrikus calmly twists his long beard threads. He caresses the white strands deliberately. A smile slowly starts to take shape.

"Excellent harlequins. My mission is done!" Zeetrikus says before vanishing in a cloud of smoke.

In a snap, we are all back and in the middle of the San Marco square. The white envelope is right in front of us.

There's just a little problem with it; it's floating in the air. I try to grab it but just when I close my fingers it slips away. When I try again, the same thing happens; soon we are all looking like fools grasping only air when we try to grip the slippery envelope.

"How predictable, Mr. Zeetrikus acting again."

"Guys, let's focus not on the problem but on the solution," says Breezie.

"I think I know what to do," I say all excited, "let's form a circle around the envelope and use our sticky fingers power." Reacting quickly, we surround the floating envelope and start to close the circle.

"Have you guys noticed that the envelope only zips and zaps sideways?" I say as we are now tightly bunched around the elusive envelope.

"Extend your palms in front of you now. Don't try to grab it!"

Our circle of hands leaves virtually no room for the envelope to move. Next, without moving my hands I make an imperceptible move towards it with my middle fingers. The envelope reacts and by moving sideways and it immediately runs into Checkered sticky hands.

"Well Done!" Is the fading voice of Lazarus Zeetrikus in the background.

The envelope reads "Holding Grudges." Exhilarated, jumping up and down, we all high-five each other in celebration.

"Time to open the envelopes," I say.

Checkered opens the first envelope, "Honesty" and reads it in earnest,

"The crossing starts where you least expect it. But you'll only find it if you follow that what you've acquired in your quest. Only compassion will lead you to the Grand Canal."

Contrary to Prague, this time we know better not to try to decipher the clues before we're ready. Experience tells us that the answers will come to us in due time.

With an air of playful mystery, Reddish opens and reads the second envelope, "Holding Grudges" and reads it with enthusiasm,

"Trust not what you see but what you step into. The only way forward will require a leap of faith from one of you. Once you all find out who it is; trust and patience will be required."

Chapter 6
Seeking Advice from
the Ancient Time Machine

The slight bump in my shoulder signals the arrival of Thumbpee.

"You all now have the ability to hover if the situation requires it. But for it to work you'll have to visualize it first. Ah! One more thing; only one of you at a time will be able to use this power," The diminutive man says before vanishing on an instant once more.

This time we know what to do next. Without a word, turning around and in tandem the 6 of us march towards the other end of the square. The full moon is now high-up in the middle of the night sky.

We continue our fast walk. We all need to have a chat and seek guidance from The Orloj. That's when the familiar buzz of Buggie flapping his wings makes itself present. Our next strides are met with an even more intense buzz. The next few with a frantic one. Finally, I stop, and the others follow suit. Buggie's tiny laser is pointed to the sky ahead of us. But none of us sees anything. Then in rapid succession, something else happens.

"Did you see the shadow that zoomed right by our backs?" A nervous Firee asks.

"No! Don't scare me Ok!" Says an equally tense Reddish.

"Yeah, there it goes again and it's lightning quick," Says Firee all excited. But only he's seeing it.

"Guys let's become invisible," This time is Breezie whispering for all of us to use one more of our powers, 'Thoughts only as well, Guys,' he adds already communicating in the form of thoughts.

We continue to walk in tandem and finally see what Buggie was pointing at. Just 30 yards ahead are two large black nets suspended in the air.

'Hard to see in the middle of the night if one doesn't know in advance,' I mull over.

'It's a trap! look at the ropes sustaining them,' Breezie says.

As Buggie's laser marks the supporting lines we turn left walking around the suspended trap-nets. The sudden swoosh of air comes to halt just short of the nets.

The hideous and short man looks extremely angry.

"Where are these slippery youngsters? they were just here," says a very frustrated dwarf.

The six of us remain motionless as the gnome zooms around the square in short bursts of energy. The gnome lets the nets - meant to trap us- fall to the floor. Folding them in disgust the dwarf makes a long chirring sound; his teeth are tightly clenched; his neck veins seem about to explode. The gnome is soon gone, cursing non-stop. Once more he has failed to throw us off from our quest's course. Remaining invisible, we walk in pins and needles towards the astrological clock at the far end of the square. None of us is certain whether the dwarf is still lurking around or not.

The piper's magical tune is faint at first. We see him entering the square with a procession of colorful characters. There's a juggler riding a single-wheel cycle, an acrobat doing forward and backward flips, an equilibrist riding a giant ball.

A crowd follows, everyone is laughing. There's joy in the air. There's music everywhere. Good things are about to happen.

"You can now come back to your visible selves," The Orloj thunderous voice catches us by surprise.

No soon we do it, Thumbpee pops up on my shoulder and Buggie's annoying buzz signals his hovering presence as well.

We all relax and smile finally feeling safe, even if it is just for a short while.

"Harlequins, time is of the essence, how can I help you?" The time exacting machine asks.

"Sir, we are struggling every time we have to decide whether to use our powers or apply wizardry." I say.

"The six of you are doing a great job. This time around is tougher though. Your decision-making abilities and your good judgment are being tested every step of the way. Additionally, throughout your quest the human virtues and flaws you've learned in Prague could be required at a moment's notice for you to understand the situation and chose the right path," The Orloj explains.

"What about the dwarf, sir," asks Breezie.

"What about it?" The time exacting machine says.

"Is there anything you can give us advice about the gnome?" Firee asks.

"In relation to the dwarf, I can't tell you how or what to do. I have no control over him. After yourselves, he's the one individual who can hurt you the most during your quest, so, confront and deal with it. Things in life are often tough and dangerous," The ancient Clock adds.

I swallow hard and tense at the thought. My fellow harlequins' expressions reflect equal concern and dread.

"Well youngsters, it's time for you to go on, time is ticking away," The Orloj says before growing silent and inert once more.

"Stay the path," says Thumbpee before vanishing as well. Buggie on the other hand draws our attention with a brief loud buzz. I

t then hovers forward, and we eagerly follow.

Chapter 7
Journey into the Unknown

When we turn the first corner, our tiny flying Buggie's laser is pointed to an arched stone entrance. It's totally dark. Once we step in, Buggie's gone. We are now on a dimly lit corridor of big stone walls and floors. At the far end, there's a set of descending steps also made out of stone, curving in circular fashion. As we go down, a humid and damp smell impregnates the air. Next, different sounds start to bombard us. First, we feel the proximity of water drops, splashes, small waves crashing; then we hear the wind howling; next come faraway laments. The wailing sounds come to us from everywhere. It's creepy and puts every one of us on the edge. That's when the ground underneath starts to growl. Instinctively, I place my hand on the stone wall for support as if trying to lean on it, but it is scalding hot.

Suddenly, some of the stair stone-steps slide inside the wall. In their place, we can now see dark empty spaces. As we continue to descend the stairs, now, we take nerve- racking little hops to avoid them. Then it occurs in an instant; Greenie takes a little step to avoid a missing step, but the step she's supposed to land on slides away into the wall. It all happens in fractions of a second and she has no time react. With no surface underneath she falls right through the gap; darkness swallows her on an instant.

I react out of pure instincts, "Hover," I'm able to shout as the last of her disappears. Seconds go by. The utter silence is ominous to a terrible calamity. Then in magical fashion, she floats out, hovering over the empty space. Her facial expression reflects terror and incredulity. "I visualized it, and the fall was broken on the spot," she says her voice trembling.

We gather ourselves and find comfort in each other's proximity. Once calm has been restored, we continue descending with little hops between steps. Whenever the situation repeats, our power to hover allows us to avoid another fall into the void. Then the circular wall starts to spin making us dizzy. The speed of the rotation increases until we start to lose focus on our steps.

'Guys, use your power. Separate fantasy from reality. None of this is real,' I think for everyone to hear.

Sure enough, the empty steps and the spinning wall disappear as we all focus on reality and discard fantasy away. The distant laments though, do not end. We finally reach an underground water channel. The wailing sounds are more distinguishable; now they come from both sides of the water channel tunnel. The familiar water-splashes of an oar-helm combo signal a gondola approaching. The distinctive sound of Venice's stylish canoes joins the tunnel's cacophony and eco-chamber of the water tunnel sound-mix. When it emerges from the shadows to our great surprise there isn't anyone navigating the gondola. It appears to be piloting itself. When in front of us it stops.

"Hop in harlequins," says the familiar feminine voice we hear.

We all recognize Lucrecia Van Egmond in an instant. She has literally materialized upon arrival. Who knows, perhaps she was always there. Our motherly antiquarian is of medium height, her threaded hair is white and long. She has pale skin, an aquiline nose, and milky blue eyes. She dresses ultra-conservatively in clothes from another era; she's wearing an ankle-length skirt and a long-sleeve blouse.

With her at the helm, we navigate through a labyrinth of underground water channels. They are poorly lit, so we notice right away countless bright pairs of tiny dots; they are everywhere. Also, when closer to the tenuous gas lamps, we can also see the shadows. Thousands of eyes are staring at us from the shadows.

"You are safe with me," Mrs. Van Egmond says as if reading our minds.

Her comforting words make us feel more at ease though not quite enough.

"Here we go," she says as we approach a storefront with a small dock.

Up closer we see the sign. It reads,

"Van Egmond Antiquarians"
(Est. as old as this city is).

Curious and excited we disembark and follow her inside. As we enter the store, the first things we see are cookies, cake, and a jar of milk.

"Help yourselves. I already know that you feasted in grand style at the house of Levi. Yet you did not have any dessert," she says with warm and loving words that make us feel safe and protected for the first time since we started our quest earlier in the night. Dutifully, we engulf in rapid fashion all she'd laid out on the table.

"Youngsters as we did in Prague, together we are going to take a short trek. This time it won't be into the backwoods; it'll be a journey back in time. Follow me please."

Once more she leads us to the back of her store. When she opens the exit door, the blurring air signals a portal.

"Ready?" She asks.

We all nod as she is already on the move. Promptly, we all walk behind in tandem.

One by one we step in, not having a clue where we are going. The brightness of the day blinds us. Right away we can feel the marine breeze. Squinting I open my eyes and realize that we are back in San Marco square, but in the middle of the day. As I look closer the place feels different. The buildings are newer, but the square floors are filthier, and the foul odors are much stronger. The waterfront is clogged with hundreds of boats of all sizes and shapes. The port activities are bustling. Merchandise of all kinds is moving in and out of the vessels in a sea of chaos and noise. But it is the people where the most notorious contrasts can be found. Most women are wearing enormous, uncomfortable dresses. Many are also dressed with gloves and hats. Hand and faces are essentially all that is exposed. On the other hand, men are dressed in ridiculously looking clothes. A large number are dressed in shirts that have greatly oversized shoulder pads, but the funniest part is that countless of them are wearing tights!

"Harlequins, we are now in the year 1295 (the end of the 13th century). Venice is the most important city-state in Europe. Today we're going to witness a theater play in open air; the stage has been set right at the port. It's about the return of the great Venetian traveler, Marco Polo, after a very long

journey. He left Venice with his father and uncle when he was only 17 years old; when he came back the great adventurer was already 42 years old. He traveled through
what are nowadays: Palestine, Turkey, Iran, Hormuz, Afghanistan, Pakistan, India, The Silk Road, China, Mongolia, Vietnam, Malaysia, Sri Lanka (Ceylon), The Black Sea among others. As spectators, we are going to experience through the actors' words and actions, the powerful human virtues of perseverance and grit," the gentle lady antiquarian says.

"Mrs. Van Egmond before we get there, could you talk to us about the meaning of the words perseverance and grit? None of us understands them well enough," Asks the eternally curious Reddish.

"Of course, my dear. I thought that once I mentioned it, any, or all of you could be interested in the subject, here is a reading that describes Grit," she says.

We form a circle around her right in the middle of the square, just before she starts to read to all of us in earnest,

"Grit"

Grit provides "lasting" quality to endurance and resilience.

Grit is that unbreakable resolve, driven passion
resolute behavior, unstoppable intensity
overwhelming fortitude, perennial discipline
indomitable courage, tenacious firmness
and unbreakable resolve
that turns us into deliberate super-achievers
and perennially likely winners.
Grit is where the edginess of a driven character, resides.

Grit is where the "unyielding determination"
to withstand fear, fatigue, privation, sickness, endless repetition,
failure, rejection, sickness, tragedy, and pain, lies.

"In relation to perseverance, let me read you another old scribble on the subject," she says just before continuing to read aloud,

"Perseverance"

The sustained action regardless of circumstances,
the continued pursuit and advancement until completion
are the trademarks of the perseverant person.
Perseverance is indefectible persistence
unrelenting steadfastness, immutable continuance.
perennial diligence, indefatigable stamina
stubborn doggedness, and obstinate insistence.

The perseverant person never deviates
from their plan, course of action, or goals,
never tires, abandons, or quits,
overcomes every obstacle, always gets back-up
and infallibly gets the job done.

Startled we contemplate her. Satisfied with our facial expressions she leads the way in the direction of the port at the far end of the square. When we arrive in front of the stage, we encounter hundreds of spectators. We then see a heavy-set man, with a humungous red beard, walking over a plank off a merchant ship.

"Harlequins pay close attention. A street theater play is often closer to reality," she says pointing to a banner with the name of the play. It reads,

"The Greatest Journeyman that ever Lived"

The rumor has spread all over Venice. The great journeyman is coming back home. An immense crowd has gathered at the San Marco square waterfront. Finally, the merchant ship coming from Constantinople makes its entrance and docks. A plank is immediately extended. Soon, a Burly man with a long red beard crosses with little quick hops the wooden platform and touches the ground in his birthplace and hometown for the first time in 25 years. Numerous relatives have gathered among the crowd.

"Venice at last!" He declares.

"Oh my god it is you! You've grown into a man," says one of his aunts with a proud voice.

"We thought you were dead, Marco," says an aunt overcome by emotion.

"That's what I thought on many occasions as well," Marco Polo walks surrounded by family and friends. He contemplates the familiar sight and feels immediately at home.

"Nothing has changed," he says with a thunderous voice.

"Much has changed Marco Polo; our current rulers don't like Venetians. But tell me, you must now be a very wealthy man?" asks an uncle.

"In knowledge and experience yes. But I've nothing else to account for. We were robbed in Trebizond of everything we earned and saved through the years."

"It means that you've come back home a poor man?"

"To the contrary, I am a very wealthy man," Marco Polo affirms.

"How come? Explain yourself," Presses an uncle.

"I have vast faith, knowledge, and experience. Those are the only true components of non-material wealth."

"But without riches, you won't be able to acquire a comfortable life, clothes, or other amenities."

"Of course, I will because my faith, knowledge, and experience will open all doors for me,"

"Didn't you encounter many dangerous situations?"

"Countless. The Tatars do not like merchants, so our encounters with them were always dangerous. Also, at the court of the Emperor of Mongolia, Kublai Khan -whom I served for decades- there were many powerful members of his inner circle that didn't like foreigners like us.

"Marco Polo how were you able to make it through such a long journey?"

"Through Perseverance and Grit,"

"Tell us what each one of those words means to you please,"

"Perseverance is how we continued forward despite difficulties and seemingly insurmountable obstacles. The thought of not completing the journey never crossed our minds. Our grit was the strength of our resolve and determination to reach our destination and complete our mission. Only when we arrived back home moments ago, our journey became successful."

"If you were serving a powerful Emperor, how did he let you come back to Venice?"

"Because he concluded that I was the only person he could trust to deliver a Princess to Persia."

"And did you?"

"Yes, I did. Once my mission was accomplished, I headed home."

"Have you written any diaries about your travels?"

"Whatever I had was lost along the way especially when we were robbed. I intend though to find a writer to whom I will narrate the entire experience."

"Your journey will be remembered as a great adventure."

"Indeed, it will. In a way what we did is no different than life itself. We are all embarked on the journey of life. Yet in order to succeed and be happy we always have to keep our goals in mind and always complete our mission. And in order to do achieve our goals, two of the most crucial components are perseverance and grit."

Mrs. Van Egmond contemplates with benign eyes our expressions of awe and wonder. We have all understood very clearly the importance of perseverance and grit in our lives. In my case, I wonder whether the actor we just watched perform Marco Polo was the real journeyman or not. When I look over at Mrs. Van Egmond, she seems to be reading my thoughts. An almost imperceptible smile and a wink follow.

"Wonderful. Just wonderful. Congratulations are in order. Harlequins you have successfully mastered the noble virtues of perseverance and grit. I am sure what you've just learned will accompany you for the rest of your lives," the gentle antiquarian says. Next, she hands the white envelope to Reddish, it reads "Perseverance and Grit."

Mrs. Van Egmond walks us back to the portal and we all step back through it and into her store. She then hugs each one of us and just after that she's gone. But nothing happens.

"We are still at her place, why?" Points out Greenie. Still inside her store, "we face two choices," she says continuing.

"Guys, we either go out of the store and hop back in the gondola and continue to navigate the water-channel tunnels or we use again the portal at the back of her store," I say.

"Isn't that going to throw us back to Marco Polo's time?" Asks Greenie.

"Perhaps yes, perhaps, not," Reddish replies.

"Why one and not the other?" Asks Checkered.

"Because none of us wants to go back to the tunnel," says Firee.

"Before we try the portal, there's no way to know if that is the right decision to make," Breezie says.

"How?" Asks Firee.

"First of all, it's Mrs. Van Egmond's portal. We've only used it at her direction in Prague and now here. It's natural for us to like it. Because at present is the easy way out. But in our quest, that is precisely what we must avoid," I say.

Reluctantly we all step out of the store dreading being once more on the water tunnel. We hop into the gondola and start paddling.

"Look," says an excited Firee.

We turn around and Mrs. Van Egmond's storefront has vanished, leaving just a humid and musty stone wall instead.

"Even the small dock is gone," I say.

The slight bump on my shoulder signals Thumbpee's arrival, "you guys now have the ability to breath under water," he says vanishing in an instant.

Chapter 8
The Gnome's Turn

Our gondola begins paddling by itself. If someone is at the helm -and it seems like it- we certainly can't see it.

As we make our way through the dark underground channel, we see a corner ahead of us; right after we make the turn, a streaming current coming from another channel joins us. Our pace is much faster now; our way forward accelerates at a rapid pace. Not feeling safe any longer, we all get a hold of anything within our grasp; on the next turn, we join an even stronger water flow. We are now in the equivalent of a water rapid -subterranean in nature. - The intensity of the current forms short and small waves. At breakneck speed, we ride up to the crests of the waves, then slide down even faster. Muffled cries come out from each one of us. The turbulent waters are now saturated with foam and whirlpools. Then we hit the first small waterfall. This time we all hit the floor with panicky screams, the sudden drop knocks the wind out of each one of us. We slide even faster as the front end of our gondola crashes into the water; we hear and feel the wood structure crack as if it's about to break. The tip of the narrow boat pushes up and resurfaces. Lying on the floor, we are being thrown to all sides; crashing with each other or the benches. We are all soaked from head to toe. The underground water- channel waters are suddenly calm. We advance smoothly yet we are shivering. We have not quite put ourselves back together when we see a massive hole in the water a water-twister rotating a warp speed, it soon swallows our canoe. In an instant we find ourselves spinning and rotating faster than clothes on a drying machine. Water circulates at a frantic around us. It is now a wall that encircles us. With the high rotation we all feel dizzy at first then one by one lose consciousness.

When we wake up the gondola is self-paddling gently through smooth waters.

"I told you that sooner or later, I was going to get you," is the voice we can hear in the background from the darn gnome, "And I am just getting started."

Still dazed, we try to come to our senses. In slow motion a dense fog engulfs us; the poorly lit water tunnel turns our nebulous surroundings into near darkness. There is an eerie silence in the place; a cold breeze blows making all of us tremble. Instinctively we get a hold of each other. The five of us are on the edge of our seats.

Then it hits me. 'Guys, go invisible now!' I think for all the others to hear.

As we all do, I have a sick feeling in my stomach though. Something is amiss. It was just a brief glance. I have to make sure.

'Reddish,' I mull. No response. 'Where's Reddish,'
Silence. Nobody knows.

'I believe I saw only the tail end of it. It happened too fast. I'm afraid she's just been snatched away!'

'What?' reacts a frantic Greenie 'Oh my...she's not here. But she was…just a moment ago,' frantically Greenie mulls aloud.

'Shhh...stay quiet,' Breezie warns us.

We only see the shadow hovering slowly around our gondola. But the piercing pair of eyes in the darkness is unmistakable.

Incessantly darting back and forth. Pure evil bursting out of them. The dwarf still can't see nor find us, he huffs and puffs as he circles around us. Suddenly, the tunnel lights up and the fog is gone. Hands on his hips, he floats in front of the slowly moving gondola with a contorted face. In slow motion we see him hover away searching the channel waters. He seems to be retracing the way we came from.

'He thinks we are on the water,' I mull.

That's when we see her. Reddish is hovering over the water. The dim glow around her tells us right away that she has become invisible as well. Only we can see her! Excitement builds up.

'Sh... guys,' Breezie reasons reminding us to keep our emotions in check.

We successfully avoid blurting out any words. Reddish in the meantime gently places herself next to me. Right away she starts to tell us what happened, 'as I was about to turn invisible, the dwarf grabbed my arm, yanked me out the gondola and threw me into the water in a separate tunnel. Instinctively I let myself plunge into the water. Once under I became invisible, went up, and once on the surface, I hovered.'

'He's turning nastier and nastier,' I think.

To the right side of the gondola, we see a dry tunnel.

There's no docking area, it's just a hole on the tunnel's walls.

'Let's hover out of the gondola, one by one,' Firee reasons.

'Wait a minute guys, how do we know is not a trap,' thinks Checkered.

'We don't know. How could we know?' mulls Breezie. 'Of course, we do, if we want to; let's check if it's fantasy or reality,' I think.

Immediately we see that the tunnel entrance is not such but the entrance of a jail cell.

We all look at each other and think the same in unison, 'the dwarf!' then I add, 'He's determined to trap us one way or another,' and the other five respond in tandem once more 'Yes, he is!'

We continue to navigate. From the back, we hear the now customary cursing and yelling of a very frustrated gnome.

The music notes first come to us as a faint rhythmic sound; soon different melodies resonate through the tunnel.

In front, now we see a curtain of water falling directly in front of us. As we pass through it, we get soaked once more from head to toe; right after we enter a massive underground chamber and are suddenly hit with lights and colors so intense that at first, they blindside us. Then, a miniature community of perhaps a long city block comes into view. There are docks and small pedestrian streets on both sides. They are framed by Venetian architecture, consisting of three to four story buildings with faded pastel colors. They all have beautiful flowers pots and lush greenery hanging from their balconies. Everyone in the tiny village is partying with intent. Some dance to the sound of the accordion, piano, and flute; further away another group listens to a magnificent trumpet solo performer; then in the middle of a small square, a larger gathering is delighted with a violinist and a cellist play as companions to a beautiful soprano. Plenty of patrons sit at the outdoor tables of several small eateries.

"They are all translucent," Checkered says.

"What else to expect, right?" I reply.

"Ghostly wizards from beginning to end of our quest," Breezie points out as we disembark and become visible again.

As we walk across the small main plaza, I spot our most eccentric mentor and book antiquarian; she's a sea of contradictions; the same beautiful but angry face; jet black hair, and deep-set green eyes yet short and hunched. I point to the balcony, and everyone notices. There she is, our mentor Paulina Tetrikus the antiquarian with the short fuse. She's wearing the same Victorian red dress we first saw on her last year in Prague. We react quickly and disembark but, in an instant, she is gone! But we know better; patiently we wait until -same as she did last summer- she pops up on another balcony. This time we simply follow her choreography of balcony vanishing acts across several buildings until she finally waves seemingly noticing us for the first time.

"She's seen us alright," I say.

"She actually did from the moment we arrived, I think," says Greenie.

Our feisty antiquarian settles on the balcony of the largest building in the subterranean village. Carefree we all run in her direction. The building has an ample atrium and a wide set of stairs. Sprinting we climb up until upon reaching the first floor we see her store sign,

"Tetrikus Antique Writings for the Spirit and the Soul"
(Est. as old as this city is)

"Harlequins, what a pleasure," she says without looking at any of us in the eyes.

"Mrs. Tetrikus, we have all been looking forward to meet you," I say on behalf of everybody.

"Me too. Congratulations are in order. I've been observing how busy you are laboring through your quest," she says showing a faint smile -something completely against her deep-rooted instincts of grumpiness and bad temper.

"I'm very pleased with your progress," she says while walking pensively. "But while at it, you must never become complacent," she says with now a stern look. "Yet, there are many things still for you to learn. Today in particular we are going to explore the virtue of Loyalty. To understand and learn how to use it well, will dote you with the keys to wonderful things in life like unbreakable friendships; rock-solid family ties; phenomenal leadership skills and integrity of character among others," she proudly says.

Still thinking and mulling it over, our eccentric mentor, antiquarian Paulina Tetrikus walks deliberately slow to the bookshelves in the far end of the store. Moments later she heads back to us with a voluminous book and starts to read in earnest...

"The Four Orphans Girls from Vietnam"

The four girls from Ho-Chi-Minh City
grew up in a shelter,
a place modest
but at the same time clean, strict,
and filled with love and attention,
in other words, a heaven for children without a home.

*The childhood friends played, ate, slept together
ever since they could remember,
and they attended class at the same public school
six days of the week.*

*Their walks to class
were memorable every day.
Holding hands, shouldering their backpacks,
they ran into numerous children not as lucky as them.*

*Some looked hungry
and they shared their snacks with them,
others seemed lost with their ragged clothes & broken sandals
to those they brought loose clothes
they'd found at the shelter.*

*Already 12, Hahn was the oldest among the foursome
by two years.*

*In the cold winter nights of the rainy season the four of them
cuddled together in bed to feel warm.*

*Hahn loved to read to them
until the younger three fell asleep.*

*Through countless children's books
the Vietnamese war orphans dreamed
about faraway places, fairy tales, fairy godmothers
princes in white horses and happy endings.*

One good day Hahn made like she was reading,
But in reality she was reciting a tale

she'd written earlier for her three friends.
There was an important reason why she did so,
an important secret only Hahn knew.
Thus, the tale she narrated that day
contained a hidden message
for her three childhood friends to uncover
something Hahn wanted them to never forget.

The story Hanh wrote and recited that night
was about a shipwreck
on a remote and barren island of the Pacific.
After a few weeks, the captain, and his crew
were starving and hopeless
as their location was so remote
that not a single ship had crossed the horizon
since their arrival.
The captain decided to risk it all and on one of the 2 lifeboats
they had been able to save,
with the help of his crew,
built a small mast and fit a small sail to it,
sewed with by the vessel's handyman.
With some of the food that was left
and water collected from the rainy days,

the captain and one crew member
set sail into the vast Pacific Ocean.

All his intended destinations
were more than 1000 nautical miles away.

Before leaving he made a promise to his crew,
"I will come back to rescue you all."
The captain and his fellow crew man navigated for 6 weeks,
they plowed through calm and heavy seas,
some were scorching-hot dry days,
others were plagued with never-ending storms.

When the captain reached land,
he worked feverishly to secure his crew's rescue,
and even though it took him a long time
he never stopped until
he found a boat to go back for his crew.

Almost three months later,
when they had almost given up
thinking that their captain had either perished
or simply saved himself and had forgotten about them,
right in the middle horizon
the crew saw a vessel arrive.

Soon they saw a tender approach
with their captain aboard waving at them.
He had never forgotten them.
Loyalty to his crew was as strong as theirs to him.
He had come to rescue them.

When Hahn finished reciting the story,
her three friends were all still awake
with big wide and intense eyes of wonder looking at her.
Cuddled together they fell asleep one more time,
wearing placid and happy faces.

The next morning
when the three younger Vietnamese girls woke up,
Hahn was no longer there.
Their initial surprise and sadness only grew when the
orphanage director informed them that Hahn had been adopted
by a Japanese couple from the city of Nagoya.

The pensive threesome headed to school that morning
in a somber and sad mood.
This until they suddenly looked at each other,
all thinking exactly the same.
"She will come back for us,"
they said in tandem with big broad smiles.
How naive their thought if they only knew?
How could a 12-year-old afford to come to their rescue?

Months passed
and Hahn letters started to arrive.
She was enjoying a very nice life with their adoptive parents.
She had picked up the Japanese language in no time.
At school, she was excelling
and was enrolled in the gifted program.

Her three friends wondered
if with so much happiness and wealth
Hanh will end up forgetting them.

More months passed
and Hahn letters described one success after another,
a growing feeling of lost hope
kept creeping up on the 3 young Vietnamese girls.

"Maybe she's not coming back for us after all,"
they would comment.
But the story of the captain and the rescue of his crew
always prevailed in the end...
"She will. There's no doubt. She will come back for us."

Then one good morning as the three girls walked to class
a shiny black limousine drove next to them.
Surprised they turned
as one of the dark tinted window glasses was lowered.
It was Hahn!

Totally caught totally by surprise,
the three young girls covered their faces.
They were at a loss for words,
Overcome with emotion, they jumped up and down
seeing their childhood friend back,
"I told you that I was going to come back for you,"
Hanh said with a voice filled with joy.

The door of the limousine opened
and their older friend jumped and ran towards them.

They embraced, hugged, kissed, yelled, and screamed
in a state of exuberant happiness.
They did so seemingly forever.

The foursome was back together once more.

"How did you do it?"
one of her three childhood friends asked,
"Ever since my arrival I worked non-stop
to get all of you adopted as well.
I earned it through my school performance
and being such a good daughter

that I convinced my adoptive parents
-now yours-
how hard-working and talented Vietnamese girls are."

When she's finished Paulina Tetrikus' face -for a change- is filled with emotions and tears. We all contemplate our antiquarian mentor with expressions of awe and wonder.

"Harlequins, loyalty is one of the most powerful virtues to possess," she says, "but tell me, what did you learn from this fable?" she asks.

"Being loyal to others is being faithful and reciprocal to the unconditional love and trust they bestowed on us by others," says Greenie.

"On the recipient's end, it's knowing and remembering that there's someone out there perhaps a few or even many that always have our back, no matter what," says Breezie.

"You never leave behind your loved ones or the members of your team," adds Checkered.

"Excellent! You have now mastered the virtue of Loyalty. Good luck and don't lose sight of your goal," she says while handing a white envelope to me that reads, "Loyalty." As I turn around to thank her, she's already gone, and we're back to the main square of the tiny underground village.

The thunderous sound takes us by surprise. Both of the water tunnel entrances on the sides of the small enclave are shut down by massive steel bars doors. In the background, first we hear the strident laughter, followed by "What are you going to do now Harlequins, there's no way out,"

'Guys the key is to react quickly before he has even made his pompous entrance in here,' I think.

'What to do?' replies with a thought Reddish.

'Use our powers' I respond back staring directly into the water channel.

'Which one? oh I see, you think there is a tunnel under

water?' asks Reddish.

'I do. So, we might as well try. Guys let's jump right into the water and become invisible once underneath.

We all start running and jump into the water. The gnome is right on our tails but stops short of the water's edge and remains hovering over it. His face is contorted with anger. The dreadful menace remains motionless observing the water where we landed. But once again he can't see a thing.

We swim under the surface with ease using our power. Sure enough, ten feet deep we see a submerged tunnel. Without hesitation, we enter the tunnel and swim with the current. After a few hundred yards the underwater tunnel's direction shifts upwards. Gradually we start to see light ahead of us, as we continue its intensity increases. Finally, we reach the surface and the first thing we see is the sun rising in the horizon, a new day is beginning. We have surfaced right at the landing -the quay- that precedes the steps to enter the San Marco Square. Amazed we simply climb up to the main "Piazza" (square) from the water's edge. No sooner have we have adjusted to the light and surroundings, Thumbpee makes himself present on my shoulder, "You all now have the power to become other people of your choosing with one caveat, it'll be on appearance only and not on a permanent basis, in fact, it will only last for a very short time," the diminutive man says remaining -for a change- on my shoulder.

We all look at each other, shrug our shoulders, and smile in complicity.

As usual Reddish curiosity prevails. "Guys we've got two more envelopes," she says and without asking opens the one that reads "Perseverance and Grit"...

"Perfect timing will be required but it will not be obvious to you at all. The north star will be your guide but at times following it will challenge your better instincts."

Next, Greenie opens the second one labeled "Loyalty" and reads with gusto…

"Sometimes you'll have to go up in order to go down and you will have to go right in order to go left and vice versa. Also, the path ahead of you at some point will be interrupted, it'll be entirely up to you to decide what is the best option ahead of you. Always remember, if you jump with intent only a leap of faith will take you to the other side."

We all smile in complicity as once more we don't understand the clues whatsoever. Yet we know that we have to be patient and in due time they will all not only fit but will be absolutely necessary for our final quest.

Chapter 9

One More Encounter with the Burly Man

Let's go and see The Orloj, we can certainly make good use of his wisdom at this point of our quest," I say.

As we stroll across the square, the early morning sun and the temperature continue to rise. Buggie joins us as he usually does for these occasions. Once in front of San Marco's square astrological clock, we wait for the ancient time machine to come alive. But nothing happens. That's when we hear the fake coughing trying to draw our attention. That's when I recall and smile while turning around. There he is, sitting on a coffee table having breakfast, the burly man with big, round, rosy cheeks, and a greased twirling moustache.

"Welcome harlequins, don't you remember that this is me during the daytime?"

All of us now staring at him nod in delight.

"I see you are making great progress, congratulations! Now, how can be of help?"

"Sir, why aren't our harlequin clothes not changing to street clothes like they did in Prague?"

"That's an intriguing question. In Prague that was kind of a crutch to help you discern the situations you were facing. Call it a compass, here and now you don't have such luxury," he replies.

"Why a crutch, Sir?" Asks eternally curious Reddish. "Well, because if suddenly you were back wearing your street clothes, that meant that you were straying away from finding one of the antiquarians, to the contrary as long as you were on your harlequin clothes, it meant that you were genuinely working and getting closer to find the antiquarian you were looking for, besides you were not wizard apprentices yet. In here you need to use your incipient knowledge of magic in order to advance."

"Thank you, Sir," I say.

"Well, let me caution you, from now on, things are going to get a lot tougher for you." the time exacting machine says.

We all swallow hard. Chills run through our bones. We are all wearing deadly serious faces.

"Youngsters time to go. Time is of the essence," he says with a perfunctory tone of voice. Our meeting is over.

We wave goodbye and leave with concerned faces. As we stroll through the San Marco square, we have no idea what is waiting for us next...Thankfully, from the moment we take our first steps I a

m both restless and fully alert of our surroundings.

Chapter 10
Above the City Known as La Serenissima

Guys we are sitting ducks in here," I say.

"What do you mean Blunt?" asks Breezie.

"Well, it's actually quite simple. This is the first place where the dreaded small man will look for us," I say.

Everyone nods in realization, "What about if we become tourists right now," I say.

"Students on a European summer trip," Greenie says. Each one of us picks a different look. "Ok let's have a seat on the street tables of the "Gelateria (Ice cream parlor) right ahead of us," Firee says.

No sooner have we ordered our gelatos (ice-creams); a swarm appears in the sky. Our nemesis the dwarf is hovering over the square with what appears to be a small army of dwarfs.

"Are those nets they carry?" asks Reddish.

"He is determined to trap us one way or another," says Greenie.

"As the Orloj said, it's going to turn nasty out there," I say.

The dwarf hovers around the square for a long time. It flies several times right by us but doesn't stop.

Under his command, all the hovering gnomes and himself deploy their nets letting them fall until de ground's edge. Then on a tight straight-line formation, they lift them to create a massive hanging net. Then they start to canvas de square.

"He is going after our invisible selves," says Breezie, "besides, our ability to impersonate others will not last much longer; Remember what Thumbpee said that it'll only last for a short time," he adds.

While we tepidly try our ice-creams anxiety continues to grow on all of us.

"I say we go high, let's use our sticky fingers and climb to the rooftops," everyone nods, "guys, we have to get moving. Let's go!" I say.

"First, once the dwarf makes the next pass, we become invisible," Checkered says.

The hideous gnome hovers one more time observing everyone in his sights including us. Once he hovers forward and has us on his back, we all become transparent. Suddenly his head turns, and we see his piercing eyes staring at our empty table. He's just figured it out, thankfully just a fraction of a second later. We are already on the move by the time he reaches the gelateria (ice-cream parlor) tables. We can hear the dwarf cursing and swearing while we start to climb -with our sticky extremities- the walls of the Palazzo (Palace) Ducale. Once we reach the roof, we are graced with a magnificent view of Venice's city line. The water channels seem like the arteries, the gondolas like tiny dots moving through it. The colors of the city paint everything with an aura of art and beauty.

"Look over there guys," says Greenie.

Not far we can see a shining. It comes and goes. At first, I think it's a glass or even a mirror reflecting the sun's rays. But it isn't so; the bright spot dims up or down in a totally random fashion.

"Let's go over there," Firee says.

"How are we going to do that? this time we don't have the Prague spires to catapult us from one roof to another,"

"If we jump with intent, -a leap of faith- will see us to the other end," I recall aloud.

"I'll go first," I announce as I start marching towards the roof's edge closest to the shining spot.

Without thinking any further, I run towards the roof's edge. As I approach the void, I try to convince myself that I'm able to jump the 20 or so feet separating me from the other roof. But the moment I plant my feet to spring myself, I know that I won't make it to the other side. Right off the ledge, I begin to fall, "Ahaaaaa..." Down I go, dropping like a stone.

'Hover now! Blunt,' I hear Firee in my head, not only ordering me what to do but also bringing me back to my senses. Halfway down I finally visualize it in my head. Right away, my fall is softly broken as I transition to floating calmly in the air, 'Guys, I could have used my sticky fingers at any time,' I think for all to hear. But it sounds more like a hollow excuse and sure enough our feisty Iberian catches me -literally- on the fly, 'C'mon Blunt, you were almost on the ground, these are not the tall buildings of Prague, you were contending with only 5 stories before crashing out. Besides, I did not see any effort from your side to use your sticky powers,' she mulls over for everyone and my absolute embarrassment. Slowly I hover upwards until I am leveled off with the roof-top and my sternly looking fellow harlequins. So, I quickly abandon the futile exercise to look for excuses and get back into action.

'Guys, the jumping power won't work unless you truly believe in being capable of executing the leap. You have to visualize it first. In other words, with confidence, picture yourselves making it to the other side.' I think for everyone.

I hover on top of the roof and place myself gently next to my 5 fellow harlequins.

'Who's going first?'

No reply is heard but I see Checkered running towards the edge of the roof. She jumps and immediately seems to be floating in the air in slow motion, 'she believes,' I reason for all to hear. A couple of seconds later, she makes it to the neighboring palace's rooftop. Soon everyone else follows one after another, 'you all got it,' I mull. Of course, everyone but me.

'What about you Blunt?' challenges me Breezie with a thought.

I look silly and petrified.

'Blunt, simply hover over here,' says Firee.

'As you regain your self-confidence, you'll have plenty of opportunities to practice in other jumps,' says Reddish.

'Besides, we don't have much time,' says Greenie.

'Remember, only one of us can hover at the same time," thinks Checkered from the other side.

Now all of them have spoken. That's what I call team effort! And hover I do. Embarrassed and all, I fly myself over to the place where everyone else landed. Before I've settled or even asked any questions, they are all jumping to the next roof, one by one.

"What the heck!" I say aloud and simply go ahead and try it myself. This time I'm relaxed and all I think is that I'll make it to the other side. I don't allow myself to think about anything else. My fellow harlequins observe my flight with expectant eyes and posture. When I stumble my way into the other roof and then roll all the way to my fellow harlequins' feet, they all laugh at me. But it's a laughter of great relief. From then on, we enjoy ourselves, and our age as roof-hoppers atop the splendorous city made out of 118 islands, always on the brink of being submerged under water. As we approach our intermittently shining target, once again the familiar light weight on my shoulder signals the arrival of Thumbpee.

"Of the approximately 3000 solid streets of Venice, you guys have been wandering above the most famous of them all. "The Marzaria" is the preeminent shopping street in town; it runs between the San Marco square -where you started your aerial acrobatics- and the famous Ponte Di Rialto (The Rialto Bridge) which is the direction you are heading at present. Having said this, I must confess that I am totally confused by your hoping activities," he says.

"Why?" I ask him while turning and twisting my head just to have a glance at him.

"Because I don't understand what is your plan or the path you are following? I am not even certain you know where are you going? Am I right or not?" The incredulous spec of a man asks.

"The truth is that we don't know either. We are just chasing an intermittent shinning spot just ahead of us," Reddish says full of exuberant and carefree ingenuity.

"If you don't know where to go, why don't you ask for help?" He scolds us.

"Perhaps we are just being infantile and trying to do it by ourselves. Obviously, that's a mistake. So, Thumbpee please tell us, are we off track?" Breezie asks with a touch of sarcasm and truth at the same time.

"It depends on which prism you look at it with. In a way you are -if only by luck- adhering to your path. But in another, you aren't, and, in that sense, you are so far off target that it's a recipe for failure," Thumbpee adds.

"So, what do you recommend Thumbpee?" I press him.

"Best is for you to start this part of your quest at the "Arsenale" (The Arsenal)."

When I turn again to ask another question, my Lilliputian conscience is gone once again!

"K, guys, we've got to find that place."

That's when we hear the opportune but still annoying buzz of our second guide, Buggie. Its tiny green laser beam is pointing in a totally different direction than the one we are heading to. As a matter of fact, Buggie's pointing backwards, slightly left from Plaza (Square) San Marco
-where we came from. - We start hopping from building-to-building following Buggie who seems to be in a hurry.

Ahead we see the bay area. We are approaching the city limits. As we hop one more time over the rooftop of an old Venetian four stories home, we face a threesome of one large and two small water-enclosed areas protected from the bay open seas, they are filled with boats of all sizes.

As usual Thubmpee's voice comes out of nowhere, "those are called "Darsenas" (docks), as you can see, nowadays they serve as docking spaces but in ancient times they served a slightly different purpose," he says cryptically as if talking only to himself, "let's go and take a look how was it then; Harlequins follow Buggie," says Thumbpee who -as usual- is unexpectedly back on my shoulder.

Buggie is pointing to a set of buildings next to one of the two smaller Darsenas. As we jump towards the target, right in the middle of our flight, blurry air in front of us signals a portal right on our path. Unavoidably we all cross through it. Thankfully we do so cleanly, but as soon as we are on the other side of it, we are all caught by surprise; the landscape has dramatically changed. The three Darsenas are now occupied by countless of strangely looking large wooden boats.

"Those vessels are called Galleys," adds Thumbpee.

"What does that mean?" Firee asks while totally lost.

"Let me explain, you see the small holes on each of their sides, those are because they are propelled by hundreds of oars as well as sails on those masts," says Thumbpee, "The docking area next to the factory, called the "Darsena Di Arsenale Vecchio" the dock of the old Arsenal factory, as you can see is filled with Galleys, that is because it is the place where the vessels are launched into from the "Arsenale" (military factory)."

But the biggest surprise for all of us are the buildings of the "Arsenale" (military factory), they are gigantic in size.

"Harlequins you are now in the presence of the facilities of what was in the 12th century, the first assembly factory ever built by humans," the diminutive man says.

"Jeee, how big are those buildings," I ask amazed by the sheer size of the "Arsenale" factory site.

"2 miles of walls to be precise," replies Thumbpee, "Let's go inside."

Once in, the place is immense and packed with massive Galley vessels in different stages of construction. The laborers' clothes reflect the era. There is a multitude of colors, sandals, and hats none of us recognize except for knowing that they are ridiculous and old. In particular, the workers' size captures our attention. They are all rather muscular but way short. Before I blurt an unnecessary question, I remember that the average human height has grown significantly over time.

"How many people work in here?" Breezie asks.

"16,000", The spec of a man replies.

"That's a lot in a single manufacturing place, even by the modern world standards," says Firee.

"Indeed, it is. Remember we are in the 12th century and this place builds one Galley per day: an entire warship every 24 hours. They will do this for 100 continuous days as all these ships are for the war against the Turks," Thumbpee adds.

The tiny puff tells me that the little man is once again gone without affording us the opportunity to ask him anything further.

"Guys we are in a strange environment we know nothing about. They don't even speak Italian here but Venetian. There's slavery in here as well. So, we better become invisible, climb the walls of this factory, and look at everything from above, right now!" suggests Breezie spit firing the words.

Soon we enjoy a clear perspective of the vast production facility. Multiple Galleys are in different stages of construction.

"Has any of you figured out yet why are we here? What are we supposed to do or accomplish?" The eternally curious Reddish asks.

We all look at each other with puzzled and lost faces. "Well, that's what we have to find out," I say trying to sound convincing.

We move through the walls using our sticky extremities. The activity is frantic. Wood is being cut and shaved all over. We can see multiple Galleys in different stages of construction. Some are just skeletons of wood. As we move through the walls the structures take shape. The more advanced ones have walls, subsequent ones have masts.

"Is that a harlequin?" asks Greenie all of the sudden.

I just see a brief glance of an intense blue color that disappears inside a vessel. There are a couple of harlequins - one dressed in red, the other in yellow- entering and disappearing on an instant into another vessel's lower deck. We nod in agreement and descend to the ground level and begin following them until they reach the last Galley and climb it using our sticky powers. The boat is finished so it's being rolled out over wood logs. Once on deck we find the place empty, we reach the lower cabin's door and tentatively enter going down a few steps one after another. Again empty. We see another glance of the yellow harlequin go down one more set of steps; it must be a 2nd deck further below. We follow filled with curiosity. The place we reach is bare; there is nothing on it but benches and the tip of oar's handles that stick out from holes on the vessel's cask. No one is in the room.

Suddenly the place goes totally dark. We feel the vessel rolling into the "Darsena" (the dock), when it enters the water, the Galley floats easily on it. When the lights come back, we look at each other in horror. We are all shackled to the benches.

'The dwarf,' I think, and everyone nods in resignation.

Pained and sickly men come down the steps, a brute of a man -a tormentor- follows behind. He holds a menacing whip, each of the unfortunate prisoners has leg irons which are clearly cutting into their skin. We are relegated to the back corner of the room meaning we are going to be witnesses of the vessel's oarsmen at work. But we are not prepared for what is about to happen.

'I recall that these boats were powered by slaves?' thinks Greenie with panic on her thoughts.

'Is that what they are?' she asks.

'I've finally trapped you smart boys, let's see what you do this time to liberate yourselves,' says the Gnome. But all we hear is his voice. So, we really don't know if he is in the vessel or not.

As the boat sails, we can see the thin blurry air curtain that cuts through the entire ship as it moves.

"Another portal guys. But this time the entire ship is going through one right now!" I notice.

"Where do you think, this vessel is crossing to?" Asks Reddish.

"I don't know, but I'm sure we're about to find out," I say.

The noise, yells, and screams signal a conflict outside. We seem to be in the middle of a war. The sounds of the swords clashing or cutting flesh signal the fact that the enemy is on our battleship. We can hear the thunder of warriors fighting on board the ship. The tormentor lashes slave after slave commanding them to row. We contemplate in horror the abuse of the oarsmen slaves. They are all still too young to have the strength and stamina to last on such a job. The oars seem so heavy on their hands and when rowing they struggle with every push and pull of the oars.

"What to do?" Asks Checkered.

"We have to do something, but what?" Asks Breezie. "Let's keep our goal in sight. Whatever we decide to do, it must include the target of our quest."

"Thumbpee and Buggie betrayed us," says Breezie out of the blue.

"What are you talking about?" I ask.

"They sent us into a trap. It was a set up. They betrayed us." Breezie argues.

"No, they didn't. We did this to ourselves. When we failed to become invisible at the factory the Gnome spotted us," I argue back.

Everyone comes to the same realization. It's our fault, "have any of you asked yourselves, how is it that none of us is behind the oars? And the slashing does not include us either, why?" Firee asks.

"Shut up and do your job!" says the tormentor to a slave that looks younger than any of us.

At that moment two warriors fall through the steps. They are dressed like the slave's master in fighting gear. Their heavy swords fall to the floor. Two short and stocky men come rushing down the steps with swords on hand and wearing totally different gear made out of metal and head shields. They first point their swords to the fallen warriors then one of them turns their attention to the tormentor.

'Guys, I've got an idea,' I mull over in a rush switching to thoughts.

'What now?' asks a totally anguished Reddish.

'Let's impersonate the warriors that just came in, visualize their clothes, they'll believe we're part of their army!' I think. On an instant we're dressed like them -turns out to be Turks we learn later- right at that moment they notice us. At first startled, they nevertheless react swiftly when they notice us in shackles. With a massive sword pointed to his throat the tormentor does as told and unshackles us. The two warriors then get busy shackling in our place the three captured soldiers. They keep glancing at us with surprised faces.

'They must be guessing that we were prisoners of this Venetian Galley,' says Breezie.

'Guys next time they turn their backs on us we all go invisible,' I think already discerning the path ahead of us. The next time one of the two Turk warriors turns around he's in shock. He pats his companion who turns as well and is equally surprised. As we climb the steps, the last sight we have of them, are their totally confused faces as they don't know what happened to us.

'You all hurry up these guys will be coming up this way in a moment looking for us,'

We run into a tumult of warriors fighting, is an out- of-control and chaotic scene. Stepping up sideways, leaning against the walls, we work our way up to the deck level and there the scene is even more surreal. It's a full moon night, and we're surrounded by countless boats engaged in warfare with each other. The sea seems to have no more space for battling ships.

'Guys we have to act quickly, otherwise we are going to get hurt,' I reason for everyone to hear.

'Blunt is right, although no one can see us, there are arrows, bodies, and swords flying all over the place, so is bound to happen," Firee says.

'Use your sticky fingers and go up the masts or lines supporting them' Breezie says.

In an instant, we are high above the waterline. Immediately we can see the magnitude of the naval battle taking place. There doesn't seem to be a clear winner. Most ships seem to be filled with Turk warriors attacking Venetians.

'Look,' Breezie points.

A couple of Venetian Galleys are retreating and making their way out into the ocean.

'Jump,' I say.

'What?' ask a couple of puzzled harlequins.

'In order to return to Venice, we need a vessel heading back,' I say.

One by one we leap from our vessel to the closest one leaving. Once safely on board, the place is a mess with countless bloody and severely wounded warriors. We not only go up high up to the masts staying out of the way but also remain our invisible selves. Soon we hit the open ocean and are on our way back to Venice.

'It'll take several days, this is not a short ride, right?" asks Reddish.

'Well, the most important thing is that we got ourselves out of that situation. But the answer to your question is most certainly yes. We have to navigate the Mediterranean past Greece and up north of the Adriatic Sea to make it back to Venice,' Firee says.

'But we came here in no time,' says Greenie.

'That's because we went through a... guys look ahead,' Breezie says pointing to the ocean to a huge rectangled area of blurry air, 'we came through a portal, and that's the one,' Breezie continues.

'Let's pray that it is the same,' says Reddish. 'We are going to miss it,' I say.

Everyone realizes that the heading we have will have us pass right of it.

'Breezie, Firee, come with me,' I say.

We descend back to the vessel's main deck. I lead Breezie and Firee to the pilot driving the big wooden helm. I grab a piece of cloth tied to a mast line, those normally used to gauge the wind direction.

'Breezie, you are the quickest of us three. I want you to use this cloth and from behind by surprise cover the pilot's eyes with it. Tie it up tightly. The idea is for him to let the helm loose for just enough time so Firee and I can steer the vessel towards the portal."

We walk in pins and needles towards the helm of the boat. The portal is approaching fast on the left side. Breezie's agility comes into full display as he's behind the pilot's back in a matter of seconds. He brings the piece of cloth around his face and is ready to proceed.

'Guys what are you waiting for, get next to the helm,' Breezie thinks with impetus.

We do as told. Then it all happens too fast for comfort. In a swift move, Breezie wraps the cloth around and ties it up tightly. As expected, the pilot takes his hands off the helm in disgust. Without seeing, he yanks the cloth on an angry move. He turns around to find the culprits but sees no one. He searches behind the wooden boxes around him. This brief instant is enough for Firee and me to get a hold of the helm.

'Just a slight change in direction,' I think for Firee to listen. And that we do but in the wrong direction! The Galley is now moving further away from the portal. We are about to cross next to it. 'Sharp turn, now,' I say. We pull the helm in the opposite but now the right direction. This time we yank the helm abruptly and that brings back the pilot's attention to us. The vessel in the meantime has turned into a diagonal line towards the portal. The pilot takes back control of the helm and at first, does not know how to react. He looks at the firmament looking for the boat's position relative to the stars.

He realizes the mistake in direction as the vessel is barely making it across the portal on a diagonal line. In the brief moment it takes the pilot to correct course, the
vessel is already through the portal, back to daylight, the present, and entering Venice's "Darsena" (dock) next to the "Arsenale" (Military factory) where we started. The pilot and crew seem totally oblivious to what has just taken place. Standing outside of the massive factory we don't know exactly what to do next.

'We are the only ones aware of all of these sudden reality changes,' points out Reddish.

'We better remain invisible, this is a totally hostile environment,' I say.

'We have to do it anyhow,' Checkered says pointing out to our harlequin clothes.

'We were told from the beginning that impersonating others will only last for a little while,' I say.

'Blunt, just to remind you, we were just wearing enemy outfits,' says Reddish.

'How do we go back then?' Asks Firee.

'We have to take the same portal in order to go forward in time,' I say.

'How do you intend to do that, is in the middle of the air in between the place where we landed and the roof-top of the four stories-high village in the distance,' says Breezie.

'That's not a jump. How do we go up?' Greenie asks. 'Simple guys, we hover,' I think, and everyone nods with enthusiasm.

One by one we hover up. The next one only follows after the other has reached the roof and confirms it. One by one we traverse the portal without incident. Once we are all on the rooftop of the old four stories-high villa, we have Venice's beautiful skyline in front of us.

"In a way you are -if only by luck- adhering to your path," I say repeating Thumbpee's words when he sent us to the Arsenale. "Our previous target was right, just in the wrong order," I say.

"The intermittent shining light?" Asks Reddish.

"Right, let's go!" I say.

We hop back from rooftop to rooftop above the city called "La Serenissima" (the most placid of all). Sure enough, soon we see the intermittent light in the distance as we retrace the same path above the famous shopping street called the "Marzaria". At the end of the pedestrian street, we descend into a larger than usual arched bridge across the "Grand Canale" (The biggest waterway in town). The intermittent shining light is positioned on the side of it, on top of a large barge in the water.

'Thumbpee called it "Il Ponte di Rivoalto" (the Rivoalto bridge),' Reddish says.

We walk inside the covered bridge, and it is populated with small shops. Right in the middle of it, a man plays the accordion with gusto. Intrigued and filled with curiosity we approach to listen better the beautiful melody. The musician is quite eccentric. He has all kinds of nervous energy, mainly tics and involuntary movements. He's extremely skinny and tall. His eyes are puffy, and he has a mat of wrangled curled chestnut hair. His clothes are ridiculously big and loose.

I look at everyone and we all have the same idea in mind.

"You are Morpheous Rubicom, we all recognize you, you can come back now from your latest disguise," I say.

The musician doesn't respond at first. But slowly a tiny smile starts to form on his face. The face suddenly morphs right in front of us and Voila! our mentor antiquarian makes itself present.

"How did you know so quickly?" He asks now with a broad smile across his face.

"Although your face features were different. Every other aspect of your character and behavior is the same," Reddish points out.

"Besides Mr. Rubicom, we were already fooled once by you through an impersonation in Prague, fool me once..." I say.

"Welcome then. Follow me please," Carrying his accordion he walks towards a tiny shop. The back door leads to metal stairs enclosed in a see-through cylinder. He waves us to follow. As we descend in circles underneath the bridge, we can see that there is a large barge moored at the end of the stairs. When we hit the barge's deck, to our great surprise what we see is a "floating" Antique Bookstore. The store sign reads,

"Rubicom Antiquarian, Books about Wealth, Fame & Love"
(Est. several generations ago).

Our mentor antiquarian leads us into the store, and we find the same layout and book distribution we first saw in Prague. There are thousands upon thousands of books scattered all around. The scent of old leather and paper is spread all over.

"Harlequins, there are a couple of guides of yours that are very upset at the moment," Mr. Rubicom says.

We all look at him with incredulous eyes.

"Harlequins, do you know what is worse than betrayal itself?" He asks.

We shake our heads displaying ignorance.

"A false accusation of betrayal," he says.

"Thumbpee and Buggie?" Reddish asks.

"Yes!" Our mentor says.

"We made a mistake," I say, and everyone agrees.

"That's for you to solve with them but do it asp."

We nod again.

"Mr. Rubicom, why did we have to go to the Arsenale first?" Firee asks.

"It was necessary to test your good judgment while in use of your new powers," He says smiling.

"And did we, do it?" Checkered asks.

"I must say that I'm very impressed. You "literally" navigated very dangerous waters unscathed. Congratulations!" says the perennially nervous antiquarian. "There was a little wrinkle though," he says throwing caution into the conversation.

We all look at him expectantly. But I know exactly what he's going to say. I'm lost in thoughts vaguely feeling the "floating" antique bookstore movements.

"You guys thought for a moment that Thumbpee and Buggie had betrayed you," he adds.

Those of us that did show apologetic faces. The others are simply uncomfortable.

"I have selected a very special scribble about the subject. Allow me to share it with you," he says as he opens a manuscript and starts to read in earnest...

"The Young Soprano from the Mountains of Merida"

*The Young Soprano's voice
is the voice of an angel.*

When she sings at the foothills
of the "Los Andes" mountain range
the little birds around her sing as well
mimicking her tune, her melody,
they form an impromptu chorus filled with the sounds of nature,
made right out in Heaven.

When the young Soprano sings
the mountain flowers bloom in happiness
the skies become bluer, clearer,
and the clouds part ways in joy
serving as the amphitheater of nature
further enhancing the acoustics
of her splendorous voice.

When the Young Soprano's voice is heard
the waterfalls, creeks, rivers, and lakes
celebrate as their trickles, roars, and splashes
display crispier, more harmonic, and crystalline sounds
that further enhance
the improvised nature's orchestra.

The Young Soprano's talents

are her ticket to the National Academy of Music

in the capital city of Caracas.
Very few make it into the famous school,
but she is surely meant to be one of them.

For weeks, months, and years the Young Soprano studies,
trains and prepares, working day and night,
harder than most, more than anyone.

Her life-long mentor, with long white braids,
a benign face, and a former Soprano herself,
gently guides the Young Soprano
as she grows and becomes a better and better performer.
Best of all, the knowledgeable tutor
knows the young Soprano more than anyone else, even herself.
In the days where dark clouds obscure the spirit
and render inutile the immense talent of the Young Soprano,
the stern hand of her middle-aged mentor
quickly restores reality
and pulls the advantaged singer out of the dark holes
she sometimes tends to fall or place herself on.

"What troubles you today, Isabella?" Asks Theresa, her mentor.
"I have difficulty trusting anyone," The young Soprano responds.
"I know dear. I know.
But what about me, don't you trust me?"
"I guess I do,"
"Why the hesitation?"
"No, no, sorry. Of course, I do."

"Isabella, your mom's sudden illness
and unintended departure is nobody's fault
and most certainly not hers."

"But she left me all alone."
"You're not alone.
You've never been alone.
Your father's life is centered around you. He loves you to no end.

Additionally, you have
all your mother's sisters -your aunts- always doting on you
unlimited love and affection.

*You also have me guiding your prodigious talent and you have the
gift of your mother's voice."*

"I get all of that but sometimes I feel angry and abandoned."

*"You have to fight those feelings.
I'm sure that your mom is up there in Heaven,
immensely proud of all your accomplishments.*

*One good day,
the anticipated letter finally arrives.
Isabella has been invited
by the National Academy of Music for an interview and test
to consider her admission to the prestigious school.*

*"Theresa, Theresa!"
She yells while entering her mentor's school office.
The place is empty.
She goes to her classroom, but she isn't there either.*

*Finally, Isabella runs to the gardens
where her gentle mentor sometimes goes for a stroll.
No luck either.
'Where's she?' she mulls while walking back to school.*

*"Isabella, there you are.
I was looking for you all over the place,"
says the school principal, Mrs. Gutierrez.
"I've been running around looking for Mrs. Theresa."
"That's precisely what I wanted to talk to you about."
Isabella looks at the school principal
with alarm and anxiety in her eyes.*

"She was taken to the hospital an hour ago."

"What happened to her? Is she alright?"
"She's sick Isabella.
She wants to talk to you, go and visit her right away."

Isabella walks and runs to the only hospital in town.
Her face is inundated with tears.
Her entire self is saturated with fear.

When she reaches the door of her mentor's hospital room,
the knot on her throat grows by the minute.

The first sight of the weakened and pale image of her tutor
leaves the Young Soprano speechless and in shock.

"Isabella dear, it is so nice for you to come,"
"Came the moment I heard, Mrs. Theresa."
"Dear, I've not been doing well for a while.
I'd hoped to get better and spare the worry to all,
especially you.
But things have not turned out the way I expected."

"Mrs. Theresa you are not going to…?
Are you going to leave me? You can't!,"
says Isabella crying and sobbing.
"Come here my love. Come," Theresa says.
Hesitantly, Isabella approaches her convalescent mentor.
They embrace and hug seemingly forever.

"Isabella, I want you to promise me that you will go to Caracas,
have a wonderful interview, and secure your entry
into the National School of Music."
"No!"
"Why?"

"Without you, I can't do it. It's over. My life's over."
Shaking her head in refusal,
Isabella stands with her arms crossed
and an awfully contorted face.
That is when she sees her mentor cry profusely.
It's a cry filled with pain,
and it jolts the Young and Talented Soprano to the core.
That's the catalyst that makes her snap back to reality.

The Young Soprano approaches her mentor once more.
The hug that follows is warm and comforting.

"Of course, I will, Mrs. Theresa. Please forgive me.
It was just a tantrum of mine."
"Oh Isabella, you have no idea how happy you make me.
Though you still have to work hard
in overcoming the trauma of the loss of your mother."

"I promise I will, Mrs. Theresa."
"Well, let's get down to work then.
I have to prepare you for the interview.
I also have to write
a detailed letter of recommendation for you.
Without it, it is unlikely that they'll admit you."
For several days straight, they work together
at the Young Soprano's mentor's hospital room.
They toil for hours and hours at a time,
until Mrs. Theresa deems her mentee ready.

"Dear, tomorrow we'll rehearse one more time
and you should be good to go after that."

But those are the last words
the young Soprano ever hears again
from her beloved mentor.
The next day when she shows up at the hospital,
she's told that her mentor passed away the night before.
At a loss at first, then utterly angry,
the young Soprano turns around and heads home,
where she locks herself up in her room.
And does not leave for days.
She even stops singing and vows to never do it again.

Finally, her father knocks at her door.

"Isabella, I'm heading to your mentor's funeral.
You have to show yourself up over there
and pay your respects.
Mrs. Theresa gave so much of herself to you.
You owe it to her."

"I'm not going!"
Nelson, her father enters the room
and faces his daughter with a stern face.
"Why on earth will you do that?"
"She failed me."
"How can you say that?"

"She abandoned me."
"No. She didn't.
She was very ill and passed away.
She didn't want to leave you.
God took her away dear,"
he says while hugging Isabella.

"Yes, she did.
Exactly like mom did,"
Isabella says aloud
as she begins to cry inconsolably.
"Why don't you get changed,
we have to get going,"
her father says stepping outside.

Without uttering a word, Isabella does as told.
Minutes later they head together to the funeral.
At the funeral, her deceased mentor's own daughter,
Megan, approaches the young Soprano.

"Isabella, just moments before she passed away,
my mom asked me to pass along a message."

Puzzled, Isabel listens attentively.
"She said: Tell Isabella not to forget
the promise she made to me."
Isabella gives Megan a half-smile of respect
while she drags her father out and leaves in a hurry.

"Isabella, the interview is the day after tomorrow,"
"Father, I want to go but is pointless."
"Why?"

"My tutor betrayed..."
"What kind of a word is that, Isabella!"
Nelson says interrupting her in disgust.
At that moment Isabella finally realizes
that she's been accusing and blaming
her loved ones for the pain of losing them.

"I'm sorry dad.
Of course, she didn't betray me.
Mom didn't betray me either.
That's wrong for me to say.
The reason I won't go
is because Mrs. Theresa couldn't
get to write a letter of recommendation
for the National Academy of Music.
Without it, is unlikely that I will be accepted."

"I see. So, what are you going to do about it?
Simply give up and quit?"
Isabella feels liberated
as if an unbearable and heavy weight
has been lifted from her shoulders.
"Tell you what dad.
I will nevertheless go
and give it my best shot.
Truth be told,
Mrs. Theresa prepared me well for it."

Isabella's interview takes place soon after,
and she succeeds in every category with flying colors.

The rehearsals of her voice go even better.

The moment of truth arrives
when she completes the last exerting evaluation.
Before leaving she addresses
the acceptance committee, one more time.

"Thank you for your interest in me.
I want you to know that I am aware
that without my mentor's letter of recommendation
I won't be accepted.
I understand this and accept it.
But next year, you can rest assured that I will try again."
She says to the Admissions Committee.

She is ready to go back home,
a bit sad but mainly satisfied that she did her best.

"Young Soprano, what makes you believe
that you won't be accepted?"
One of the members of the committee asks.

"Don' take it as an excuse
but my tutor passed away
before she could write
the letter of recommendation you require.
I came nevertheless to honor a promise I made to her."

"You came just to fulfill a promise?'

Isabella thinks long and hard.
She stares with intense eyes at her examiners.
Then decides to blurt the truth the way she feels it.

"Also, because I feel that I am ready for it."
"Ready for what if I may ask?"
Asks another member of the admissions committee.

"Ready to be admitted in the Academy
and not only succeed but also,
be one of its top performers."

"Isabella. First of all,
your mentor did send to us
a detailed letter of recommendation several weeks ago."
Says a lady member of the committee.

Emotions build up in a hurry in Isabella's chest,
her lower lip trembles,
a couple of teardrops slowly slide through her cheeks.

"Second, we would have accepted you anyhow without it.
That's how well prepared and talented you are.
You have honored the good efforts of your mentor
by fulfilling all of the admission requirements
with flying colors."

Isabella jumps in joy and hugs her father.
She politely shakes hands with every member
saying thank you to each one of them.
She then walks out
proudly holding her father's arm. "And Isabella..."
says the same lady member,

The young Soprano turns around,
"Yes?"

"Your mentor,
also said in her letter
that if you did show up
and a scene like this ever happened,
to tell you to look in your assignments folder."

Isabella quickly opens the folder
she hasn't opened for weeks.
Page after page she contemplates
the impeccable work of her mentor
until at the very back of the folder,
she sees the envelope.
"Letter of Recommendation for the National Academy of Music."
It was always there!
She realizes. When she opens it,
she finds a little note with the letter,

"Worse than betrayal
is to falsely accuse our loved ones
of such an offense."

Morpheous Rubicom contemplates us with inquisitive eyes.

"Harlequins what have you learned from this fable?" He asks

"Many of us have ghosts of the past that control our present," says Reddish.

"In relation to them, what is our job then?" Our mentor presses.

"We have to work hard to find a way to be liberated from them?" Says Greenie. "Otherwise, we run the risk of what?"

"Of being trapped inside of them forever," Says Checkered.

"What else?"

"Not living," Firee says.

"And?"

"Creating excuses like blaming others for our pain," Breezie says.

"Still missing an important one,"

"Creating and living off false memories," I say.

"Excellent. Awesome! Harlequins you have learned your lesson about the vice of betrayal well," he says while handing to Greenie the envelope. It precisely reads that, "Betrayal."

And just like that our nervous mentor disappears without another word and as he does that, we are left standing back at the Rialto Bridge thinking about what to do next.

Chapter 11
Chasing a Nordic Ghost

All of you now have the power to perceive what someone else is feeling. Use it wisely," Thumbpee says before disappearing without a word.

"He did not even give us a chance to apologize,"

"Let him be, he's hurt. I am sure he'll come around and we will get a chance to express it to him," I say.

We climb back to the nearby roofs and without a clear path, start to make our way back to the San Marco square. Once again, we've made a mistake. This time it'll have serious consequences.

"Before we get going guys, there's something we have to take care of," I say.

Everyone looks embarrassed -including me- no one is even staring at me but straight at the floor. Yet one by one nod in slow motion.

"K. Thumbpee, Buggie we need you. Make yourselves present, pleeeease," I plead.

Nothing happens. All we hear is the swoosh of the slight breeze and the paddling of the gondolas coming and going underneath the bridge.

"What do we have to do for you guys to show up?" I press.

Nothing at first. Then it comes out nowhere...

"We are here," Thumbpee says announcing himself while we can also hear the faint buzz of Buggie in the background.

"Where?"

"Right here. You can hear us but nothing else," the minuscule man says.

This time we can hear Buggie's buzz clearer; in two short but intense bursts as if validating Thumbpee's words.

"Alright then, -we understand you don't want to be seen- We want to apologize," I say.

"You want to apologize about what?" Asks Thumbpee.

Full of shame I walk the plank.
"For claiming that you betrayed us," I reply.
"Did we?" Presses Thumbpee.

"Not at all. You never did," I say.
"So why did you guys say such a venomous thing?"
"Misguided anger and misfired frustration about our detour at the Arsenale," Breezie say intervening.

"Are you awfulizing? Is that an excuse, Breezie?" Presses further Thumbpee with Buggie's rambling buzz confirming his every word.

"No, it isn't. I take full responsibility. I'm the one who said it," Interjects Breezie.

"If that is so, why is everyone taking responsibility then?" Thumbpee asks.

"Because we're a team. When one fails, we all fail," I say.

"Perhaps you all feel guilty because you didn't push back hard enough against Breezie's words," Thumbpee says now in an accusatory tone.

"As a matter of fact, we did, immediately after Breezie spoke. And we all -including him- came to the realization that everything was our own fault," I continue, this time with forceful intensity.

"So, what's the problem then? Is there any problem at all?" Asks Thumbpee with a joyful tone.

"We thought you were both upset with us. Mr. Rubicom alerted us about it," Reddish says.

"That was one more test of your good judgment by good old Morpheous Rubicom," The spec of a man says.

"And how did we do on it then?" Asks Checkered. "Passed with flying colors," Thumbpee replies.

"Are we good then?" Firee asks.

"Of course, we are, we always were. You may want to reflect though on why if there isn't any problem between us, you still acted guilty," Along with an intense buzz from Buggie, their laughter is the last thing we hear from them. A small puff with sparkling stars signals their habitual and sudden vanishing act.

"Guys let's get going, time's running out," Greenie says trying to get us out of our awed state.

"Isn't that our mentor, Mrs. Dillettante?" Asks Reddish pointing to the Marzeria shopping street underneath us. Her tall figure and blond hair in a ponytail stand out.

"She's the last antiquarian remaining in our quest," I say.

We climb down in a hurry. When we hit the street, she is already far ahead. We run after her, but she's at least a block and a half ahead. Then we see her making a sudden turn left and immediately lose track of her. Seconds later we arrive at the place where we think she went in. We are not certain though if it's exactly the right location or another Venetian palace located next to it.

"There she is," says Greenie.

"Where?" Asks Firee.

"Up there!" She says pointing upwards to a building standing right behind where we stand.

Mrs. Dillettante is now walking at a fast pace on the building's rooftop.

"What the heck is she doing?" I say as we climb in a rush.

Once at the top we see her three buildings away. Then we see her jump.

"Where did she go now?" Breezie asks.

We reach the ledge where we saw her jump. What we see is a slide used to flush out debris from a construction site. It is unusually long, perhaps a mile in distance. We see her sliding down on it at top speed towards a water channel.

"Forget about jumping, it is way too long for us to leap, besides there are no buildings along the way either," I say.

"What do we do then?" Asks Greenie.

"Slide, guys, slide," I reply.

We all hop in and are soon speeding down as well. Way ahead of us, we see her reach the end, stand up, and take the helm of a gondola tied up next to the slide. By the time we reach the end of the slide ourselves, Mrs. Dillettante is already several hundred yards away. We all board another gondola. But it is manned.

"Follow her," I say.

We navigate smoothly in front of magnificent and splendorous Venetian old palaces. Mrs. Dillettante paddles faster than us, creating a greater and greater distance.

"Can you go faster?" I ask the gondolieri.

He shrugs his shoulders but paddles a bit faster. We've only been a few minutes navigating the Venetian waters when Checkered's facial expression turns to utter fear.

'Guys, the gondolieri whoever he is, harbors deep nasty feelings towards us. I suggest we all hop out simultaneously to the next gondola that crosses out path,' using her new power she thinks for all of us to hear. We can't wait for the moment that another gondola shows up. Next, when we see another gondola docked to our left, I get into action. 'Guys go invisible just before jumping. We do it on 1, 2 go!" We all become invisible and immediately jump to the empty gondola. A couple of seconds later the gondola we were riding is crushed by a Vaporetti (an engine-powered water-taxi). The gondola sinks in a matter of seconds right in front of our startled faces.

We see the dwarf staring at the water collision. It is easy to discern that his nerves are crisped in frustration.

"Where are them?" he screams.

'Guys we can't stay here, let's get moving; remain invisible; start climbing the water channel wall now,' Breezie presses to get us out of the shock at the gnome's latest mischief.

'There's Mrs. Dillettante,' points out Checkered.

We see her walking on the other side of the water channel. She's walking two small dogs.

'Now look guys, like she did in Prague, Mrs. Dillettante is morphing,' Firee says.

While walking by the water's edge, we witness when she becomes an old lady strolling along with her two dogs. For the first time, we can stay closer to her. Then she splits into two identical selves, both walking a pair of identical dogs along the water channel's edge.

"Are you guys seeing what I am seeing?" Asks Reddish.

"Yeap we now have two of her," says Greenie.

But as soon as she finishes now there are four old ladies walking two dogs each.

"Now, I'm totally confused," says Checkered.

We speed up trying to get a closer look at the four Mrs. Dillettante specimens. They all look exactly the same to me. That's when it gets even weirder. The four ladies become six and each takes a turn in a different direction. I realize that we have to react immediately.

"Now there are seven!" points out Checkered.

"Each one of us goes after one. Let's split right here," I say.

"There is one too many, what to do?" Asks Breezie.

"It must be on purpose; nevertheless, we do what we can at the moment, we follow six of them and let one lose," I say.

"We're going to lose sight of each other, at that moment we'll maintain communication through thoughts," Breezie says.

As each one of us starts to follow each old lady, soon thereafter I lose sight of my fellow harlequins. The old lady I'm following is now walking at a fast pace. The dogs are gone. In an instant she morphs into the original Mrs. Dillettante, a statuesque Nordic beauty with her long blond hair bundled in a ponytail.

'She's just become her," I think for everyone to listen. 'Mine too!" replies Reddish.

Soon the other five confirm the same. The five old ladies they are all pursuing have morphed back into our mentor, antiquarian Lettizia Dillettante. That without the sixth version of herself which at present is unaccounted for.

'Blunt, how do we get back together?' asks a panicky Firee. I realize the predicament in a second. But as I chase our fast-moving mentor, ideas flow back, 'Our meeting point should be the square, no, we better not go there. Ok, yes, the Rialto Bridge, that's where we meet if lost,' I mull.

'Blunt, I believe the natural thing to do is to go high.

Let's all go to the roofs,' opines Breezie.

'And do what?' I ask.

'Simple, ask for help. If we want to find each other, we call upon Buggie to guide us to each other,' Breezie adds.

'Brilliant! Agreed' reasons Reddish.

In the meantime, the version of Ms. Dillettante that I'm following walks into a palace, and I follow. Inside I see her opening a door and closing it behind her. I follow and do the same just in time to see her opening another door in the far end and closing it again. This time I trot towards the door, and she's already on the other end of the room going through another door. 'I've got to talk to her,' As I get to the other end, she does it again but this time faster. Soon I become trapped in a game of doors opening and closing at warp speed, but I can never get close enough to her.

'Guys I'm chasing doors in here,' I think for everyone to hear.

'And I'm surrounded by mirrors with a hundred images of Mrs. Dillettante, and I don't know which one is real,' says Greenie.

'Well, I'm jumping from rooftop to rooftop and the jumps are getting longer and longer but I cannot get any closer to her,' says Reddish.

'Wait, wait; guys we are going about this in the wrong way,' thinks Breezie who himself was chasing Mrs. Dillettante on a gondola.

'It better be good because I'm back in a tunnel chasing Mrs. Dillettante and I don't like it one bit,' says Firee.

'She has me jumping inside of one painting after another,' says Checkered.

'I've just stopped chasing her,' Breezie informs us.

'Why?' I ask.

'She's not Mrs. Dillettante,' he adds.

'How do you know?' Asks Firee.

'I used our new power and focused and what she was feeling,' Breezie reveals.

We all react in an instant and do the same. 'Mine isn't Mrs. Dillettante either,' I mull over. Soon the other four conclude the same.

'None of the five we were chasing are her,' thinks Reddish.

'I am afraid the only real one is the one that got away,' adds Greenie.

'As agreed, let's go high and get together first,' Breezie thinks.

Buggie does his job guiding us all to the Bridge of Rialto. Reunited, we greet each other with expressions of resignation. Buggie's buzz in the meantime intensifies. His tiny green laser beam immediately catches our attention. With expectant eyes, we follow it and to our surprise, there she is sitting on a coffee table, reading a newspaper. When we're all staring at her from a distance, she lowers her reading pages and winks at us.

"C'mon harlequins follow me; we're already late."

We trot towards her. She stands and greets us with benign and warm eyes but does not say a word. Next, she swipes her hand, and a portal of blurry air immediately forms in front of us. She walks through it, and we follow.

Suddenly we are in a part of town that we haven't been to yet. Sure enough, Mrs. Dillettante has vanished again.

The slight bump on my shoulder announces the arrival of my conscience, "Harlequins, you are now on the Venice old ghetto, on it the Jewish population was segregated during 287 years from the rest of the town. So, it lasted almost three centuries from 1516 until it was finally ended by Napoleon in 1797. It is a place where not only a lot of suffering took place because of the prevailing antisemitism of the era but it was also a place where immense enlightenment, religious studies as well as intellectual and artistic work took place. Above all the old Jewish ghetto of Venice was a place filled with bonds of love intertwined with bountiful gratitude and especially forgiveness," disserts Thumbpee.

We all look at him with eyes of awe and wonder.

But the significance of the place gets to us in an instant. "Thumbp..." I start to ask but by diminutive conscience is already gone.

We walk to the ghostly place with respect but deeply unease about its historical background. The architecture is clearly Venetian but is clearly less grandiose. Its colors are also less vivid.

"A sadder Venice," Reddish reflects aloud.

As we turn the corner the brightness of the light's blind sights us at first. The flashing sign on the shiny storefront reads,

"Dillettante & Dillettante Antiquarians"
(Est. A Century and Half Ago)

It's a building several stories high. It's totally illuminated in stark contrast to the surroundings. Our tall and strikingly beautiful mentor waits for us at the door.

"Welcome harlequins. I'm glad you finally made it safely over here," she says.

We walk with her inside her immaculate store. Once more a single bench in the center on the entrance hall awaits us. Weall sit together as Mrs. Dillettante opens a book, she has obviously prepared for us.

"You didn't expect to get here that easily I presume?" She asks.

We all shake our heads.

"Well, your decision-making and good judgment in the use of your powers was put to test once again."

The five of us sheepishly smile in acknowledgment.

"In every instance, you all reacted wisely hence saved yourselves a whole lot of trouble," she adds.

She walks and paces herself calmly. Her face is serene and the smile of satisfaction she wears does not go away.

"Today we will explore the issue of forgiveness. I thought long and hard about how to best go about it with you guys. Until finally, it occurred to me that placing my store in this location of Venice was the right way to start the subject. Finally, earlier this morning I decided what reading was going to fit best our lesson. I must say that it is a story that I have revisited many times over the years. Please allow me to read it to you," Book in hand, Ms. Dillettante takes a seat in front of us and starts to read in earnest.

"The Ace Pilots encounter in the deep ends of the Rain Forest"
(Amazonia 1960s.)

"Many, many years ago,
I met in the jungle an extraordinary man
that became my best friend in life.
But things did not start well at all when
we first met each other,"
says the old man as he narrates
for the first time to his grandson
one of the key moments of his life.

"Grandpa, is this another one
of those war stories of yours?"
Asks his grandson with big wide eyes
and a voice filled with excitement.

"Yes and no.
Be a little bit patient and you'll see,"
says the many times decorated war hero.

The excited grandchild
cuddles closer to his grandfather
on the reading chair they use every night.

"It starts like this..."

Flying over the Venezuelan plains,
the battered twin engine is facing in the distance
the vast Amazon rainforest.
Straight ahead a wall of dense nature,
splashed with endless shades of green,
lazily draws nearer and nearer.
Once more the mysterious and untamed jungle
awaits the arrival of Samuel Ely Saperstein
an experienced World War II American pilot.
After flying in and out of the remote region
over the last two decades,
he feels as comfortable
with the familiar surroundings
as with the humming of the sputtering engines
and the sight of the peeling paint
of his dependable Piper Aztec.

At first, they seem like tiny obelisks far ahead.
As he flies closer, they seem like a formation of giant totems
protuberating above the treetops in the horizon.

He can now see clearly the peculiar flat-top,
vertically narrow,
pre-historical mountains called -Tepuis –
by the locals.
The ace pilot initiates the preparations
to execute the harrowing, dare-devil landing.

One he's performed hundreds of times before.
Saperstein descends to one thousand five hundred feet pointing
the aircraft to the clearing
lying atop a gigantic Tepui
in the middle of the rainforest.
As usual, he makes his first pass
above the site with his engines at full throttle.
The frequent visitor wants
the unmistakable noise to be noticed.

As he banks and turns back in the distance,
machetes on hand,
countless Yanomami Indians
emerge from the jungle and run towards the clearing.

Frantically,
they all start chopping away
the waist-high brush and foliage.

As the familiar plane makes a second pass,
the Yanomami wave at their trusted provider of vital supplies,
including medicines
and essential tools like their priced machetes,
it's their signal that the improvised runway is ready.

Moments later,
after a deft, precision landing
executed with only a couple of bounces,

within a couple of hundred yards,
the plane comes to a stand-still.

The tribe's leader, Itakere greets Saperstein
right after he jumps off the aircraft.
The long-time friends embrace while the place is off-loaded.
"Welcome back old friend," says Itakere in perfect English.
"Glad to be here."
Says the pilot.
"There's much to talk about," the tribe's leader says.
"Certainly. Looking forward. Here are your books,"
The airman says.
"Always an honor.
Your generous heart has helped me
build a precious book collection,"
The head tribe's man says.
"Always a pleasure," The pilot says.

"Before we get started
there's someone I want you to meet,"
says Itakere.

At the tribe's fire pit, a bearded man lies.
He looks sick and emaciated.
several bandages cover his extremities as well.

"He flies planes and is also a World War II pilot like you.
Nowadays, he's a river pilot.
We rescued him days ago down the Orinoco
a half a day's walk from here."

Samuel's eyes grow wide with interest. "Did he crash?"
"Yes, His floating plane into the river.
That is why he is still alive.
Because he hit the water instead of land or trees."

Hours later as Itakere and Saperstein play
one of their memorable chess matches,

the injured man wakes up.
His seems dazed
and struggles to regain focus.

When he finally sees the American Pilot,
his eyes first grow wide in total surprise
then relax at the sight
of another jungle visitor like him.

The two players take notice
and turn their attention to the river pilot.

The American pilot stands up
and approaches the convalescent man.
"Samuel Ely Saperstein,"
he says extending his hand.
"Ernesto Otto Gerlach,"
The injured pilot responds extending his.
As they shake hands,
the heavy German accent
is immediately recognized by Saperstein.
He immediately drops Gerlach's hand,
turns on his heels, and walks away,
without uttering and single additional word.

The tribe's leader is caught by surprise
as much as Gerlach does.

"Mr. Gerlach let me go and find out
what's just happened in here.
I'll be right back."

Itakere finds Samuel pacing back and forth
inside his habitual sleeping quarters.
When the tribesman approaches,
Samuel waves his hand at him in a gesture that means
both that he doesn't want to talk and wants to be left alone.
Nevertheless, Itakere ignores the rejection.

"Do you guys know each other?
Is there a problem between the two of you?"
Asks Itakere to his old friend Samuel Saperstein.

"No, I've never met him before"
"Why your reaction then?"
"He's a German and I'm a Jew, you wouldn't understand."
"Of course, I do,
not only because your books have educated me
about what happened in World War II
but also because of your attitude
is no different than the behavior
some warring factions
have against each other over here in the jungle."

The tribe's man approaches his old friend
and places an arm around him.
'C'mon follow me,
let's go and talk to your fellow airman."

At the fire pit
they find the wounded German Pilot
sitting straight with a still startled face.

Both men contemplate each other for a long time.
This until Samuel lets it go.

"All my uncles, aunts, cousins, nieces,
grandparents and childhood friends
died in concentration camps
at the hands of you Nazis,"
says panting the American Jewish pilot,
"The only reason my parents -rip-
my siblings and I survived the war
is because we'd moved to America before it started,
this because my father was hired away
by an American University," adds Samuel,
"So as a teenager I enlisted myself
and went to fight you guys
as soon I was old enough
and I did it in the sky downing as many of your planes
as humanly and physically possible,"
continues Samuel.

An uneasy silence follows
as the German pilot listens to every word being said.
His demeanor is natural,
his face does not show discomfort much less guilt.
With profound warmth in his voice,
he replies…
"I don't know anything about you, Sir,
but I feel your profound pain and sorrow.
First of all, I was never a Nazi,
and don't take this as me repeating
the typical uncomfortable but convenient excuse

often overheard in Germany
decades after the war, even today,
repeated by many
who don't really believe or feel that way.
No, in my case, I wasn't born in Germany
but in this beautiful South American Country
of Venezuela,
in the oil region of Zulia.
When I was 12 years old
my German-born parents sent me to Hamburg
to complete my high school in Germany.
They wanted me to get acquainted
with our relatives and the country's culture.
Over there I discovered my passion for flying,
so, at 14 I started to fly gliders.
Unfortunately, at 16
I was forcefully recruited
to the German air force -The Luftwaffe-
towards the end of the war
they were running out of everything including pilots,
so teenage boys like me were sent to war.

I only lasted six months flying for the Germans.
On a reconnaissance mission,
I was shot down over Poland
and was captured the moment I touched ground
with my parachute and became a prisoner of war.

Although the war ended shortly thereafter,
I spent two years at a Russian concentration camp.
I was released only
because suffering pneumonia they thought I was dying.

With a fellow prisoner equally sick as myself,
we started to walk west towards Germany.
As both of us were half-naked wearing only a pair of shorts;
on the first Polish village
they gave us shirts and sandals.
We walked all the way to northern city of Hamburg.

I found a city totally destroyed
and my relatives in disarray.

The only thing I wanted to do,
was to return to my home country. And I did,
but not before procuring myself with travel documents.

In order to do that
I had to traverse and hitchhike going south,
across a devastated and hungry Germany,
all the way to Bern in Switzerland
where at the Venezuelan embassy
I could finally get a passport.

Then I had to traverse
the whole of Germany country again,
this time going north,
then cross the North Sea until reaching Oslo, Norway.
the only place where at that postwar time,
cargo ships were still heading to Venezuela.

After a three months wait,
I finally was able to get on a ship
and made my way back to my home country,
and that was forty and some years ago.

But I never stopped flying,
and the Amazon has been my home for many years now,"
says the German-Venezuelan pilot.

Samuel's tears inundate his face.
"I am so, so, sorry, please forgive me," he says.

"There's nothing to forgive,
as you can see,
I have no feelings of guilt about World War II.
I'm ashamed for what Germany did but I wasn't part of it,
at least not voluntarily.
And the same goes as well
for the vast majority of Germans today
- especially 40 plus years later. -
Sir, although you can and shall never forget,
you have to learn to forgive them
but especially yourself,"
Concludes The German-Venezuelan ace pilot.

With profound satisfaction and proud of his old friend
Itakere sees Samuel Saperstein leaving.
Doing the dutiful with gusto and the help of the tribesman,
Samuel loads the wounded German-Venezuelan pilot
into his plane.
From atop a Tepui
- the house of the gods - in the local language,
Samuel throttles his 2 propellers at full power
for the narrowing and short take-off.
And once more
from the improvised runaway
on the flattop prehistoric mountain,

the plane barely lifts off,
brushing the top of the trees
at the end of the runway, on the way up.

From then on,
the couple of sixty-plus-year-olds
establish a long-lasting friendship.

One a German-Venezuelan ace pilot
the other an American Jewish flying ace himself,
form an unbreakable bond
that is to last for the rest of their lives.

The six of us contemplate our statuesque antiquarian. Her Nordic looks reflect the serenity of someone doing exactly what she loves. She looks at each one of us with love and affection.

"Harlequins, what have you learned here today?" She asks.

"Samuel learned that day how to forgive," says Reddish.

"What did he exactly do to achieve that?"
Asks Mrs. Dillettante.

"He was confronted with the truth," says Greenie.

"What truth?" Our mentor presses.

"That you cannot judge an entire nation 40 years later," says Checkered.

"What else?" The attractive antiquarian continues to press.

"That even among those Germans that were part of the war, there were many that were victims as well. In this case, Mr. Gerlach was forcedly recruited into the German air force and later was sent to a concentration camp," says Breezie.

"What else can you think about this fable?" Mrs. Dillettante asks.

"Our inability to forgive others blinds our mind and spirit. We can, not only make horrible mistakes under such beliefs, but we can also hurt others," I say.

"Wonderful!" Mrs. Dillettante says joyfully, "mentees, you have concluded successfully your search for wisdom on this year's quest, congratulations!" She says handing the white envelope to Checkered.

It reads, "Forgiveness."

When we turn to thank her, Mrs. Dillettante has already vanished! Reddish wastes no time and opens one of the two unopened envelopes and reads in earnest.

"The deep ends of the twirling waters hold a secret you must unveil. You'll have to conquer your fears in order to solve the riddle."

Checkered in the meantime has already opened the one she just got from Mrs. Dillettante. Excited she reads as well.

"There's a rainbow at the end of every trying and cumbersome path. Such a reward will come to you only if you keep the end in sight and avoid getting sidetracked."

Right away we receive the usual unexpected visit from my conscience. His tiny, high-pitched voice cuts through the air grabbing our attention in an instant.

"This time you will be able to use your powers during the bridge crossing on your final quest. Good luck," says Thumbpee on a brief appearance and disappearance act on top of my shoulder.

"Why this time we get to use them?" Wonders Reddish.

"Because we'll need them!" Breezie replies.

"Guys he said good luck, meaning we won't see him again until we are across the bridge."

"How do we get to the bridge? We're on an antique book shop on the old Venetian Jewish ghetto all the way across town," Firee says.

"That's for us to find out. But we better do it quickly. We don't have much time left for our 24 hours to elapse," I say.

We're left inside of Mrs. Dillettante's store all by ourselves pondering what to do next.

Chapter 12
Crossing the Never-Ending Bridge

As I ponder with the others our next move, the first clue we earned hits me like a lightning bolt; as if talking to myself I begin to recite it aloud, "the crossing starts where you least expect it. But you'll only find it if you follow what you have acquired in your quest. Only compassion will lead you to the grand canal."

"Does it mean then that the bridge could very well start right in this part of the city?" Asks Checkered.

"Exactly! We were all expecting the imaginary bridge to start at The San Marco Square. The Orloj said that we have to get to the island across the bay that is in front of the square. He didn't say though that the imaginary bridge starts at the square," I say.

"Where does the bridge begins then?" Asks an inquisitive Firee.

"Where we least expect it," mulls aloud Reddish until her enthusiasm bursts out of her, "I got it, I got it, where we least expect it now! At this moment," she says.

"You mean here?" Asks Checkered.

"Precisely. Isn't this place the old Jewish Ghetto where we will least expect the imaginary bridge to start?" Reddish reasons.

"Makes sense, but where is it? I don't see it," say Greenie.

"A bridge is generally something connecting two separate points over something else. In Venice is almost certain to be over water. So, we may as well walk over to the nearest expanse of water," I say.

We all walk out of Mrs. Dillettante store to an early afternoon light and sun. Right in front, there is a water channel called "Misericordia", so we stroll alongside. We see no bridge though. Reddish remains fixated while contemplating de metal plate with the name of the water channel. As I turn to see her, a mischievous smile forms on her face as she turns her eyes towards me.

"Guys, the word and meaning of "Misericordia" are the same in Italian and Spanish. It means compassion," Reddish says all excited, "Only compassion will lead you to the Grand Canal (Channel)," she says reciting part of the clue.

"What's the relevance of the Grand Canal? Why do we need to get there?" Asks Breezie.

"We absolutely need to get to the Grand Canal. The bridge will lead us up to Plaza San Marco. The St. Giorgio Maggiore Church is located right in front of the square across the Grand Canal." Reddish adds.

The moment she completes the sentence, a translucent covered bridge forms right in front of us and immediately starts to expand over the water and to our right.

"That's the direction of the Grand Canal," I point out and everyone nods realizing that our assumptions are dead on. Eager to begin we step into the covered bridge and begin our final quest.

"The Challenge of Humility"

The bridge's covered passage is poorly lit. The floor is made out of wood, so it cracks with each and every one of our steps.

The walls are solid, so we have no view outside of the bridge. It's a cautious beginning, initially, we barely make any progress. Even though no one says it, we all behave the same way. Seemingly, the memories of our previous "final quest" experience in Prague's Hradcany Castle's tunnel, still linger over all of us.

Right at the entrance of the bridge, the walkway turns into a set of stairs wide enough that go from side to side. I cannot see the continuation of the walkway ahead of us.

"Sometimes you'll have to go up in order to go down," I recall aloud the first clue we got.

"But this is exactly the opposite, Blunt," says Reddish.

"Remember you all, if it's absurd and outrageous, it's probably right, besides, in the clue, the word -vice versa- was used as well," I say.

"Meaning that sometimes we'll have to go down before we go up," says a now excited Reddish.

But her enthusiasm is not going to last long. The moment we start to step down the lack of light quickly engulfs us, and we are suddenly submerged in total darkness. Instinctively we all get a hold of the handrails as we step down further. Darkness is such that we don't even know who's next to each other until we talk to each other.

"Something just brushed my legs!" Says Greenie.

"What?" Asks a nervous Reddish.

Checkered who's holding my hand, suddenly squeezes it, "Blunt, there's something in front of us. I can feel it,"

"Did you hear that?" Asks a panicky sounding Greenie.

"No..." I reply.

"Guyyys! Something just brushed my hair!" exclaims Reddish.

"Shadows, I see shadows floating all around me!" yells Firee.

"We can't see a thing Firee, how can you see a anything...wait a minute I see them, they are like darker shades of black, they are moving in all directions," says Breezie.

"Something is creeping up on my neck," yells Greenish now on a panic attack.

"Ahhhh...tiny legs are crawling on my back," Scream Checkered.

"Guys...guys there's some kind of creature flapping its wings right by my left ear...ahhhhh," Firee yells.

"Calm down! I want to remind you all that we're being tested. Don't let your imagination run amuck and take control of your common sense. Ask yourselves if what you're experiencing is real or not," I say just before switching to thought-only communications, 'Of one thing we can be certain guys, right now we don't know who's listening,' I think for everyone to hear it.

'Neither do we know who's watching us; I say we go invisible right now!' Breezie adds.

'Invisible in darkness?' wonders Firee.

'Precisely the point. We can't see a thing, but we don't know who's watching us, this way we ensure that they won't be able to see us,' Breezie argues back.

'Done,' Greenie says and everyone else confirms as well.

We reach what seems to be the end of the steps. In replacement of the handrail at first, we all grab and hold tight to each other. 'We've got to move guys,' I think.

Continuing forward we now move in pairs holding hands. I can hear water drop from what I sense to be a low ceiling. The surface we walk on is wet so we can hear only the echo of our footsteps as we splash the water.

'Ahhhhhhh!' is the screaming thought we all hear from Greenie, 'The dwarf!' she thinks aloud.

I turn around scanning the absolute darkness that surrounds me. There they are. The par of evil eyes, two bright yellow dots darting incessantly in the darkness.

'Nobody moves!' I instruct, "he can't see us, but he can hear our footsteps. Stay still,' I think for everyone to hear it.

The dwarf's eyes move around us incessantly. The intensity of the gnome's stare quickly grows into obfuscation. At some point, his eyes hover right in front of my nose sending chills through my entire body. I remain motionless even containing my breathing.

The pair of crazy evil eyes start to move around us at frantic speed. They swing up and down, right, and left. Then we see the shining eyes spinning out of control, finally vanishing with a tiny, muffled explosion.

With Checkered firmly holding my hand I take a couple of steps forward until I reach a new set of stairs.

'I am climbing with Checkered,' I announce.

Everyone confirms that they are doing the same. Still, without any visibility whatsoever we begin to climb the stairs.

After a long climb back up, we reach the bridge's wooden-floor. The only thought in my head is to stay ahead of the moment. All I know is that we have to react quickly and pre-empt the situations before they take place.

'I say we go a step further and using our sticky fingers we climb the side walls,' says Checkered.

'Isn't that over the top Checkered?' asks Reddish.

'No, it isn't since as take each step we don't know what we are stepping into either,' adds Checkered.

In absolute darkness, we are now moving through the walls of the bridge, and we do this with ease since we encounter no obstacles. I am concerned with the near state of panic some of my fellow harlequins find themselves in. So, using one of the powers we earned earlier, I focus on how they are feeling. The moment I do it something wonderful happens. The colored suits are all suddenly fluorescent in the blackness of the covered bridge.

'Guys use your power to read the feelings of all others,' I think.

'Great!' responds Breezie.

'Thanks' replies a much more relaxed Reddish.

'I don't know where I'm!' says Greenie.

'I am staring at you right next to me,' I respond.

'I cannot feel the wall on my fingers!' she exclaims. 'Me neither,' Firee.

We all can see our harlequin suits but cannot feel the surface of the wall our sticky fingers are adhered to...

'Wait a minute I'm floating in the air,' Thinks Breezie. 'Me too,' replies Firee.

'I can see you rotate,' I note.

'And I can see you as well,' confirms Firee.

'Grab hands guys, get a hold of someone,' I think.

Checkered reaches me and holds my hand tightly. I know it's her because of the suit. We start to rotate in slow motion; We have no control of our movements.

'Do you hear it?' I think.

'It is like a whistling sound,' Checkered replies.

Next, it feels like we've been just thrown into a strong air current. Airborne, Checkered and I start to rotate in tight circles at full speed. It's a whirlwind. We are being sucked into the center of it. I can feel how badly Checkered wants to scream and break our thoughts only communication.

'Checkered hold on, it'll pass. If you say anything, they will know where we are."

'I feel dizzy,' she thinks, and it's the last thing I remember before I pass out.

When I come back, the situation has not changed. I am still firmly holding hands with Checkered, and we are both floating in a void of darkness. I can see two other pairs of fluorescent harlequin suits floating in absolute obscurity closely to us. Everyone is accounted for.

'Blunt, is it you still holding my hand?' Checkered asks 'Yes, I'm right here next to you,' I reply.

'Why does your hand now feel old, tiny, and full of hair?' she asks.

'Spooky,' I think.

She tries hard to pull her hand away, but I resist. 'Checkered, you have to trust me, it's my hand what you're holding, no one you're holding, no one else.'

I can feel her angst and fear. So, I tighten my grip a little bit harder to reassure her.

'Guys, use your sticky fingers and get a grip on the walls,' I say.

As we continue to move along the walls of the covered bridge, a strong smell hits me all of the sudden.

'Blunt, are you getting the same smell?' Checkered asks me.

'Yes.' I reply.

'What is it?' she asks

'It's the smell of water I believe,'

Slowly the darkness starts to lift. At first the shades of black turns into dark grey then followed by its lighter shade until it becomes silver and finally afternoon light. We can finally see each other although in a bit of a ridiculous positions stuck like spiders to the walls of the bridge roof. In a few of moves, we lower ourselves to its wooden floor. We hug each other in relief but not for long, knowing there's no time to waste; promptly we set out to continue to walk forward on the bridge. But we're in for a surprise; up ahead, the bridge turns sharply right.

There he is. Standing with his arms crossed, our trusted mentor and antiquarian, Cornelius Tetragor wearing his white robe and long beard.

"Wonderful performance harlequins. you have excelled on a very difficult challenge," he says.

We are still shell-shocked, barely listening to what he says. "In order to make it to this imaginary bridge, one of the virtues you'd to learn was honesty. Today your knowledge about it was tested once more," our wise old mentor says.

By now we have all come back to our senses and are paying close attention to his every word.

"So, tell me what else did you learn today about honesty?"

At first, we all seem lost about the question. After all, our challenge took place in a totally dark environment so, what we were dealing with throughout, was fear. We couldn't see...wait a minute...I get it.

"The number one lesson was trust," I say.

"Why?" Our mentor antiquarian asks.

"For honesty to exist trust has to be present," answers Firee.

"How come?" Mr. Tetragor presses.

"We have to believe and trust that the other person is honest," Reddish replies.

"Without trust, what happens to honesty?" Follows-up our mentor.

"It's worthless. In other words. It is not valued or appreciated," replies Greenie.

"And what's the consequence of that?" Continues to interrogate Mr. Tetragor.

"There's no reason or benefit in being honest," Checkered responds.

"So, you wouldn't be honest then?" The old antiquarian presses her.

"I would but out of my own conscience, but many others won't," she counters.

"Excellent! Now, going back to the original question, how does all of this apply to your challenge earlier today?" He questions.

"Mr. Cornelius, trust is precisely what we exercised throughout the whole challenge. We all held each other hands and always relied on each other. Later although we were not even sure whose hand we were holding, we all still continued to do so," I reply.

"Dead on! In absolute darkness, you all -literally- demonstrated blind trust between all of you. Congratulations! I have no doubts in my mind that if you continue to demonstrate de same kind of decision making and good judgment in every remaining challenge, you'll succeed in your quest to become young wizards," says our white-robed mentor before vanishing with a brief reverencing bow as a sign of respect to all of us.

"Trust not what you see but what you step into," I recite the clue that we earned earlier. Everyone nods in agreement.

"The Challenge of Holding Grudges"

The expressions of fear are almost gone from our faces when once again we start to walk forward, on the translucent covered bridge. No sooner have we advanced a few hundred yards than all of a sudden, we start to see fumes of white smoke coming through the wooden floor. Are first they are only a few and small in size.

'Guys, hold hands with a partner,' I think for everyone to hear while Checkered grabs my hand once more.

A few more steps and the fumes are coming through the walls and roof of the bridge as well. Fog now engulfs us. It's dense and allows for virtually no visibility.

'Again, without vision?' complains Breezie.

Unexpectedly, we hear the sound of not one but a couple of doors opening and closing.

'That's strange!' I react in surprise.

Once again, we hear the sound of the same couple of doors opening, but this time they do not close, or at least we don't hear it. When we take a few more steps, we see the open doors, one to our right and the other to the left side. The clean opening on the bridge walls is absent of any fog. Through it, we see the palaces of the grand canal on each side.

'Let's get out and bypass the fog. Then we can retake the bridge further ahead when there's no more left on it,' says Breezie.

'That's the logical and easy thing to do. The question is whether that's the right decision and whether that is what's expected of us,' I mull over.

'What do you think?' Asks Reddish. 'I say we continue,' it's my reply.

'But that's absurd,' complains Breezie.

But the word "absurd" resonates with all of us at once. We know that we have to continue walking through the fog. For a while, progress is slow as we move forward with great caution. Slowly visibility starts to improve until is finally gone altogether. What we aren't expecting though is for the bridge to come to an abrupt end. There's a solid wall in front of our pathway. It has a massive window with a forward view of the Grand Canal.

'There's no more bridge, this is the end of it,' laments the obvious, Firee.

When looking around the dead-end spot, we all see the ladder affixed to the wall. Atop the ladder, there's a hinged flap. Without hesitation one by one we all climb it. I go first and easily push up the square wooden flap. Once at the top, we stand on the roof of the covered bridge. Breathing fresh air for the first time since our quest began feels liberating. Front and back we have the Grand Canal. On its sides are the rows of Venice's magnificent Palaces and old Mansions. The frontal sigh corroborates that the bridge ends where we are standing.

'Let's create a portal with the goal in mind that it takes us to the continuation of the bridge, wherever that is, are we all in agreement?" I ask.

Everyone nods in agreement. Next, we need to know which of us has at present the portal-creation power. We all swipe our hands visualizing the bridge continuation.

This time the portal is created by Breezie, the only one of us at present that enjoys such power. The portal's thin wall of blurry air is formed right at the edge of the end of the tunnel. When crossing it, we all have to literally take a step into the void with the Grand Canal directly underneath waiting for us.

'The way forward will require a leap of faith,' I think for everyone to hear, recalling one of the clues we earned.

Without hesitation, we all eagerly cross the thin wall of blurry air. When stepping out though, we are back at the same place on top of the roof at the end of the bridge.

'Guys did we make the same mistake as in Prague and the portal didn't take us anywhere?' asks Reddish.

'I don't think so, turn around,' I say.

We all do, and the sight catches us completely by surprise.

A gigantic balloon sits atop the roof.

'This is how we get to the continuation of the bridge,' observes Firee.

We all board the big round basket and let loose of the lines holding it.

'Pull the handle,' switching to voice communication, I say to Breezie who's standing right underneath the hanging handle.

Breezie does as told and a short yet intense flame fires up, sending hot air to the Balloon's inside chamber. Next, away we go going higher and higher above Venice.

"Six small benches?" Asks Greenie complaining already about the tight quarters.

"Guys let's have a seat,' I say ignoring her.

Once seated we are all facing different directions. Hovering above Venice, with perfect weather; cloudless skies, and a light breeze. The views above the countless water channels are stunning. After quite a while nothing happens, and everyone starts to show signs of restlessness and impatience. Then we hear the familiar sweet and magical melody. We know the flutist is near, and somewhere present. Something special is about to happen. Sure enough, all of the sudden a floating screen forms right in front of me. It is projecting high-resolution images with vivid colors. Out of curiosity, I glance quickly and see that each one of my fellow harlequins have a floating screen of their own. When I turn around, I'm in for a shock. The face in the middle of the screen is me but much younger, perhaps 5 to 6 years old. I'm lying on the floor face down, arms and legs spread-eagled. I'm throwing a memorable tantrum simply because my father could not carry me any longer over his shoulders. I recall the moment in an instant. We were in Billund, Denmark at the Legoland amusement park. The images scrolling in front of me make me feel deeply embarrassed. One after another, images of mine either angry, frustrated, or non-cooperative, always throwing a fit to express those states. That anecdote is followed by similar incidents with teachers, fellow students, my mother, etc, etc.

The pace of the images is relentless and overwhelming, and it shows the same behavior as I grow up. I feel embarrassed and quickly lose count after a while. So many occasions always reacting the same way. I peek at my harlequins and their faces of discomfort tell me that they're going through the same type of experience. I wander distracted out of the images.

'What a contrast with the life and beauty of this city and the wonderful weather that surrounds us today. Me watching my bad behavior while I could be instead enjoying this ride,' I reflect.

Then it hits me like a thunderbolt. 'That's exactly what happens when I react angrily and hold grudges. I am missing out my own life,'

'So much wasted time!' I say aloud.

Right after I say that I realize that my fellow harlequins have been listening to every one of my thoughts and spoken words. Their guilty expressions speak by themselves. Looking at me one by one nod in agreement with my statement. At that moment something magical happens.

'Look,' says Reddish all excited pointing down at the Grand Canal.

We all witness as our translucent imaginary bridge re-emerges in the distance. It reappears block by block as Lego blocks dropping in place one after another. The silhouette of our passage spreads like a snake through the Grand Canal and into its wider part -a kind of open bay - in front of the San Marco Square. Next, our balloon starts to descend heading into the newly formed continuation of the bridge, right in the middle of the Canal. We descend softly above the rooftop of the covered bridge. When we step out of the Balloon our trusted mentor, Lazarus Zeetrikus is waiting for us, wearing his customary black duck-tale suit, and bent top hat. "Harlequins you've just watched yourselves again and again, acting out of feelings of anger in your childhood years. Although as youngsters we don't harbor yet the resentment that arises when we don't get rid of anger; nevertheless, it is easy to see the path many of us take since we are very young. It begins with fits and tantrums and soon enough we're holding grudges," Mr. Zeetrikus says as a way of introduction, "But tell me how exactly did you overcome the challenge you were facing?" he asks.

"As I watched myself misbehaving, I realized that I failed to enjoy so many things, " Adds Reddish, "today as a way of an example, as I watched myself being constantly angry as a child, in the meantime I missed much of the wonderful flight. Contrasting Venice's views and weather with my past behavior made something click inside of me. It helped me understand," she concludes.

"Understand what?" asks Mr. Zeetrikus.

"Exactly what Blunt said. Being angry is a total waste of time. Mr. Zeetrikus, I didn't really know, that I had spent so much time in my life being angry at situations or at people. So much time simply thrown away," Reddish says.

"Stay the course harlequins. Don't get sidetracked," he says and tipping his bent top hat he vanishes on an instant.

"The path ahead of you at some point will be interrupted, it'll be entirely up to you to decide what is the best option ahead of you," I recall the clue we earned, but nobody pays too much attention to me.

The truth is that we are all still rattled inside.

"The Challenge of Perseverance & Grit"

We are all left staring at each other with the embarrassed looks of those that have just faced uncomfortable truths about themselves. Our immediate problem though is different.

"We need to get back inside the bridge," says Breezie always trying to figure out his next acrobatic move.

"Do we?" I ask.

There's music in the air. There's music all around. The water trickling, the soft whistle of the wind. Once more, every sound around us feels like a melody. The magical sound of the flute comes to us again. Instinctively we turn and stare from the bridge's roof across the water channel into the sidewalk. There he is, dressed as a jester. Instead of walking he moves doing tiny side jumps. We follow him with intent. When the old wooden roof starts to crack and give way to our footsteps, using our sticky fingers and legs, we follow the flutist through the sidewalls of the bridge. This we do until all of the sudden, he is gone! We climb back up to the bridge's roof and stand on it in pins and needles. But there's still no entrance to it. That's when a beautiful white ray of light drops from the sky into a section of the roof just ahead of us. I look up and immediately recall the clue, "The north-star will be your guide but at times following it will challenge your better instincts," I recall aloud immediately drawing everyone's attention.

We walk with tender steps towards the pointed spot. The sun is already three-quarters of the way down the horizon. The advancement of the day looms large on us.

When we reach the roof spot pointed to us by the north star there is a big opening on it. When we peek to seek if it is a way to get back in, all there is to see is a black hole. We have the choice to walk around it and continue our march over the bridge's rooftop. But we know better to check the less desirable option first. We form a circle around the hole but see nothing. We stare at each other shrugging our shoulders signaling that we don't have a clue what to make of it. Then it happens: a whirlwind quickly forms inside the black hole. In no time the wind twirls at a vertiginous speed. Instinctively we all take a step backward when feeling the pull of the air current trying to suck us in. The blowing forces twisting inside of the hole in the roof become noisy as a wind turbine.

"Should I jump?" I ask aloud. "Are you crazy?" Greenie yells.

"This is the absurd thing to do," I reply.

Then without further hesitation, I simply jump. But as soon as I drop a few feet inside, my feet land on the equivalent of a jumping bed that ricochets me right back -through a small hop backward- to the roof.

"The way forward will require a -leap of faith- from one of you. Once you all find who it is; trust and patience will be required," I recite aloud one of the clues we earned. Everyone nods signaling they understand.

"Who's next guys, we have to keep trying," I say.

Brave Reddish does it. Scratch, she bounces back. Greenie, Breezie, Firee follow, same result. We are down to Checkered. This time our fellow harlequin is swallowed by the vortex of the swirling wind. Then nothing happens. Minutes go by and no sign of her. This until we see her slowly hovering up from the vortex. She wears an inviting smile.

"What are you guys waiting for, jump after me," she says.

"We all bounced before," I counter.

"That was before I did it. Try it again," she says before letting herself drop back inside the small tornado.

"Perfect timing will be required but it will not be obvious to you all. The north star will be your guide but at times following it, will challenge your better instincts," recites Checkered the clue that fits perfectly to the current situation.

We all jump one after another and this time are sucked in by the vortex of the swirling wind. I go last. The moment I enter the twister I get caught in a high-speed wind twirl. At warp speed, I go around in circles with leg and arms spread and body positions up, down, and sideways. Twisting and turning in every direction.

'Checkered, where is this heading?' I think for everyone to hear.

'Guys just hang on in there, it'll pass, I've done it twice. I'm waiting for you at the end of all of it,' she says.

The wind twirl releases me all of the sudden and I begin to free-fall. I try to hover, but it doesn't work.

'Checkered are you using the power to hover?' I ask while falling like a rock.

'Yes, I'm, so it's not available to the rest of you at the moment,' she says.

My fall is halted when I crash into freezing water. The first thing I think for comfort is my power to breathe under water. With the light of the day the water is transparent enough that above me I can see the bottom of the bridge floating on the surface. But I don't get much time for contemplation; suddenly, an undercurrent traps me. Once again, I'm twisting and turning as I move forward. Through glimpses, I realize that my fellow harlequins are going through the same contortions. On a brief glance, I see a couple of gondolas lying on the Grand Canal bottom floor. Ahead of me, I see a sunken vessel. It has a large perforation on the bow. Short of it the current releases me and my fellow harlequins. There are only five of us I notice.

'Checkered?' I call.

'Stay the course, Blunt," she answers.

I don't even get a chance to ask her anything else. The vessel's hole sucks all in. Once inside I can see that the water contained in the chamber has a surface, so we all swim up to it.

'What is this?' I ask.

'Obviously an air bubble within the sunken ship,' answers Checkered.

'Where are you?' I ask

'I told you, at the end of the challenge waiting for you all,' she replies.

'What are we doing here?' I ask. 'That's for you to find out,' she says.

'But you already know, tell us,' says an angry Reddish.

'The deep ends of the twirling waters hold a secret you must unveil. You'll have to conquer your fears to solve the riddle,' Checkered says reciting another one of the clues we've earned.

The rest of us realize what she's saying. 'Each one of us has to solve the puzzle,' I reflect.

We step out of the water in what must have been one of the cargo areas of the boat. We roam around until we see a desk full of rust from the saltwater. On it lays a giant leather -bound book. Strangely enough, the book looks pristine on the outside. Certainly not like something that has been either submerged in the water or lying around in an unkempt area. When we approach, it starts to glow. The closer we get the more intense the glow becomes. Before we open the book, it opens by itself. But both pages are blank except for a single line at the top, it reads:

"Checkered."

We look at each other in disbelief. On my own, I decide to turn the page and the next page has my name at the top.

"Blunt"

Followed by a question that reads:

"Who is the flutist?" is the question on my page.

"Why are all the pages blank but just with our names?" Asks Reddish.

"Don't you see that I have a question?" I ask. The other four look at me in disbelief.

"Ok, I get it, neither of you can see it. Reddish, turn the page," I say.

She does and the next page has her name on top but is blank to the rest of us.

"Can you read your question to us; we can't see it, only you can."

Reddish then reads it, "what does the piper mean to you?"

Then I read them mine. Next, Greenie turns the book's page and reads hers, "what does the flutist represent to you?"

She is followed by Firee who reads it in earnest, "How do you feel when you encounter the flutist?"

Finally, is Breezie's turn. He turns the page and reads in earnest, "The piper is a symbol of what for you?"

With everyone in the room done reading their questions, we need our South-African fellow harlequin so I contact her via thought communications, 'Checkered can you tell us what your question was?' I ask.

'Certainly. The flutist comes and goes like what?' She thinks for all of us to hear, 'you are getting close. Careful though, the questions can be shared but the solution is individual to each person,' she replies.

'Is there any way you can help us?' Asks Reddish.

There is silence for a while until Checkered comes through with an answer that is not only valid but also wickedly helpful.

'The answer is the same for every question,' she replies.

I think about it for a while until it dawns on me. The same happens to everyone else. Within seconds we all look at each other with complicit facial expressions. We all know the answer.

A vertical and transparent tube forms in the room. It is wide enough for a human form and it shoots right up through the roof and vessel's fuselage of the chamber we are in. Slightly above our eye level, the tube's ending is sealed and rapidly fills with water. That's when we hear the flutist magic melody again. As the familiar tune spreads around, we know that good things are about to happen. And they do, an intense halo of light starts to emanate from the tube's ending directly into the vessel's metal floor. It has the same circular shape of the tube. At first, it blindsides us. Reddish is the first one to step into the circle of light right underneath the tube filled with water.

'Spell the answer,' I ask her.

And she does but we can't hear it. The ending of the tube opens up, yet the water does not fall. To the contrary it absorbs Reddish, and we see her flow through the water upwards in slow motion. I go next stepping into the light circle in the floor, I spell the answer myself: "Happiness." I am absorbed by the tube's water as well. When I reach the surface at the end of the tunnel, the first sight I have is that of Checkered and

Reddish standing by an open door on the bridge wall. Filled with emotion, I climb the small ladder and hug my harlequin pals. Soon the six of us are together in a pile-on of camaraderie and happiness.

When we step inside the bridge, we see her. The middle-aged lady with milky blue eyes and long white-hair threads, "Magnificent harlequins, I'm so proud of you all!" says Lucrecia van Egmond our trusted mentor and antiquarian.

"Tell me, what is your takeaway from this challenge?" She asks.

"We all learned a lot more about the meaning of happiness" Reddish.

"I could clearly see that; it was very rewarding as your mentor to see it happen. Especially how you all figured out the answer on your own. But tell me, what else did you experience?" She says.

"We put into practice what we've learned about perseverance and grit," I say.

"How dear?" Mrs. Van Egmond asks.

"Throughout this challenge, we had to be persistent on our goal. While we faced one obstacle after another we never got sidetracked. We stayed our course all the way to our destination, all of these are elements of perseverance. Additionally, although all of us were constantly in fear, even terrified, those states never stopped us from continuing moving forward, or making decisions and taking chances. Also, solving the riddle involved a lot of passion from all of us and these are all elements of grit."

Mrs. Van Egmond responds with a joyful smile then hugs each one of us whispering beautiful words of encouragement on our ears. It all gives us great comfort. As in other occasions, our gentle mentor makes us feel safe and protected.

"Go on harlequins, go on. Love you all!" She says before vanishing in a cloud of tiny stars and bolts.

"The Challenge of Loyalty"

We resume our walk through the covered bridge passage with a sense of urgency. We stroll with a sense of purpose eager to complete our tasks. But we soon realize that times tics away in life always at the same pace. Ahead of us, we can see the bridge's way split into several paths. In between them there is bubbling and fuming water. We approach the divisions with careful steps; in front of us, there are six different narrow paths to move forward.

"Clearly there are one for each one of us," Breezie reasons.

"Well, we may as well find out. Easy right? Each one of us takes one," says Reddish ready to move on.

"Reddish that's too obvious. We run the risk that way that some or all of us run into difficulties," I say.

"Why?"

"Because we don't know if each one of us is supposed to take a specific one and if so, which one is it?" I reply.

"What to do then?" She presses.

"We do what's not so obvious. We all go through one at random that we all agree on. If we fail, then we all fail together. If we make it then we all make it together," I say, and everyone agrees at once.

"Let's go for a run then," Breezie says.

Following him, we pick the central narrow path. But the moment he steps into the path parts of it disappear in front of him, the same happens with the other five paths. Then something magic happens, a mosaic of patches matching the yellow color of his suit, form ahead of him, they are spread across the six paths signaling a way to the other side. He gets it and starts hopping from one to another, cris-crossing from one side to another as he jumps from one to another. We can see how every tiny colored patch disappears shortly after he's left it, but his pace is so fast that he is ahead all the way through. Effortlessly and in no time, Breezie reaches the other side. The moment he does, the entire six paths reappear back in place. I step in next, and the same thing happens, the six paths are now also the color of my harlequin suit, a mosaic of blue dots. I try my best to do it as fast as Breezie, but I don't have his ability, so I feel under tremendous pressure as the patches are disappearing almost at the same time, I jump off them. I finally make it safely to the other side and the six paths reappear back. But standing next to Breezie I worry about the girls.

"Breezie, you have to go back and help them," I say as the other 4 harlequins are frozen in fear on the other side.

Without hesitation, Breezie steps back and his own mosaic of patches reappears; it is a colored labyrinth that he covers in an instant. In the next few minutes, I witness how he guides each of the other four safely across.

With no time to waste we are on the move right away.

"Where's Breezie?" Asks Reddish.

I turn around and don't see him. But I count only four of us, Greenie is missing as well.

"Greenie is missi..." I start to say but immediately realize that there is no one around me.

'Guys, can you hear me?' I try switching to thoughts communications, but there is no response.

I'm standing alone on the covered bridge, worst of all I cannot even see my body or extremities. Nevertheless, I decide to move forward and cover a fair amount of ground in a few minutes. Ahead of me, I see a space of blurry air with the shape of a door. 'A portal?' Doubts creep all over me. Is it part of the path we are following or is it created by...'Clever. Very clever,' I mull stepping into it right away.

I'm back to the spot in the tunnel just before everyone started to disappear and all my harlequins are already there.

"Welcome back Blunt, as usual, you are always the last," says Breezie with a sarcastic tone.

"Can't help it guys. Who created the portal to come back?" I ask.

"Reddish," Firee replies.

I hug our fiery Iberian harlequin but ever so briefly. We have work to do if we want to make progress.

"Blunt we were waiting for you to decide what to do next," says Greenie.

"Thank you. Now, what do you want to do next?" I ask.

"We don't really know what to do next," says Checkered.

"You are avoiding a decision because you know that we have to go through the experience of not being able to see each other involuntarily, including ourselves. But we have to," I say.

"How?" Asks Breezie.

"It's actually quite simple, we have to hold hands until we go through this phase. We cannot let go of each other. Further, I believe that this is something we have to do for the rest of the way. Think about this, if we would have done it before this challenge, we would not have to come back," I say.

And that's what we do. Holding hands from the six of march back to the portal.

"Hold down you all, we're missing a couple of things. We don't know if we are going to be able to communicate with each other. Perhaps now will be different but that's not certain. In case we still can't, then the key is not to lose our handholding grip on each other. Additionally, let's also go invisible," I say.

"What good does it make when on that part of the bridge, albeit involuntarily we already are invisible?" Reddish asks.

"I don't know but let's try it. On this one at least, we decide to be invisible on the other we don't" I reply.

We all go invisible first then walk across the portal holding hands. Once on the other side we are rewarded with a couple of new things. Although back to being invisible to the point that we can't see each other nor even our body and extremities, we can now see our blurry silhouettes as if were made out of water.

'It worked!' it's the enthusiastic commentary made by Greenie.

'Why?' Asks Checkered.

'Not entirely sure but the natural thing to assume is that it's because we are holding hands and we are in contact with each other,' I reason.

We walk forward as our involuntarily invisible selves. The walls of the bridge now have windows and we can now see San Marco Square to our right-hand side.

'Guys, we are about to cross the shallow bay area separating the square from our destination. This is the final stretch.' I think.

Suddenly we see in the bridge windows images of Checkered. Entering the hole of the water vessel we all visited before.

'For some reason, we are being shown what happened to her while she was ahead of us,' I think for all to hear. We see her surfacing as we did inside the air bubble protecting the vessel's chamber. When she surfaces there's an old man with a long, long beard that helps get out.

"Well done Checkered, well done. You're the only harlequin that made it through this challenge,' the man says with a gentle smile.

"Who are you?" She asks.

"One of the antiquarians you have to meet. My mission is to teach you guys about loyalty," he replies.

"But I don't know you. I have never seen you before. What's your name?" Checkered presses.

"Lucius Petrificus," He replies a bit uncomfortable.

"That's a funny name. How come I've never met you before," she presses.

"I'm new this time around. The Orloj wants all of you to meet new antiquarians each time around," he replies.

"What about my fellow harlequins, what do I need to do to help them finish this challenge? She asks.

"There's nothing you can do; they've failed and are out of this year's quest. Who knows if they'll ever be invited back? But you still need to finish this challenge. The good news is that I can help you get out of here and be back at the bridge. C'mon follow me," he says.

"I'm not going anywhere without them," Checkered responds with an angry tone.

"I'm just trying to help you. Are you willing to fail and be thrown out as well?" The old man presses.

"Yes! If they've failed as you say then I won't continue myself," Checkered affirms.

"Young girl you're becoming obfuscated. You've almost made it through. You are very close to becoming a Young Wizard. You just have to trust me," The old man insists.

"No antiquarian has ever helped us to finish a challenge. We are supposed to solve them ourselves. And always together as a group. Oooh...you...I know who you are!" Checkered blurts out in realization as the old man morphs back into his real persona the Dwarf! A very irate little man indeed. He stares at

Checkered with intense eyes of fury just before disappearing in a cloud full of smoke.

Back to reality, the images on the bridge's window panels disappear and we all turn around to look at Checkered with eyes of respect and admiration.

"You never told us what you went through," says Reddish to her.

"Why worrying you all. I wanted you all to succeed," she replies with teary eyes.

"Even after we finished the challenge of perseverance and grit you didn't take credit either,"

"Perfect timing will be required but it will not be obvious to you all," Checkered says reciting one of the clues we earned earlier. We all nod in understanding.

"Checkered you demonstrated unbreakable loyalty to all of us on that occasion," I say.

"We're a team. We will all make it or fail together," she says.

At that moment we all become visible again and a familiar voice is heard.

"Also, because you're working and staying together," says Paulina Tetrikus with a big wide smile across his face.

The short and slightly hunched antiquarian with a beautiful but angry face, jet black hair, blue eyes, and a bad temper once again seems completely transformed and animated by our presence.

"Youngsters, in all the years I've mentored young wizards, you are by far my best group. You've demonstrated just now that the concept of loyalty is not only clearly understood by you all but that you've already incorporated it in your lives by putting it into practice in the direst of circumstances.

Checkered loyalty is not only unshakable it's also reciprocal, because she feels the loyalty you all have for her," Mrs. Tetrikus says before vanishing still wearing a big benevolent smile on her face.

"The Challenge of Betrayal"

The bridge's walls' glass panels continue. Now we have great views of the city from different angles. Ahead of us is a set of scattered but interconnected walls blocking the way. There are six different entrances in the form of high arches. We try to do the same and all of us go through one but each one of us is bounded by an invisible field until Greenie walks through. The rest of us try to follow her but are rejected once again. We move to the next entrance and this time is Reddish is the only one not rejected.

"Every door is pre-assigned to one of us," I say.

On the third entrance, I'm the one who goes through. The moment I walk in, the walls lead me to the left and immediately right. It is a labyrinth. Then I see the mirrors, the walls around me are filled with mirrors of all sizes. Some are from floor to ceiling. I can't see an exit or the passage I came from. At first, it's just a glance, was that a child inside one of the mirrors? There is something familiar about it, creating an eerie feeling that creeps all over me. I turn around slowly on the big mirror I'm facing, instead of me, there's someone else, staring right back. He is smiling with mischievous eyes. It is a child perhaps 4 or 5 years old. First, I recognize the clothes and the shoes. Wait a minute, it is me! Once more my lateral vision catches a glimpse of another image. I rotate my head slightly to the left and on another full-length mirror, there's a

child as well. This one perhaps 7 to 8 years old. Recognition on this occasion is instantaneous. It's me again. The eerie feeling keeps building up as I stare at more
and more images of me at different ages. I'm now surrounded by multiple images of myself at different ages, all of them projected in full-length mirrors. I notice that only one of the mirrors has no images at all. When I stand in front of it, instead of me what I see is countless mirrors in a row inside of it. For no reason other than curiosity I extend my hand and touch the mirror. The surface is cold and solid. But when I do the same with one of the other mirrors, my hand goes through with ease. Spooked, I pull it out and stare at the younger image of myself on the other side. I notice that the mirrors are closing on me, so the space is becoming smaller and smaller by the minute. My next move is deliberate, yet I swallow hard when I take it. With trepidation, I simply step into one of the mirrors. On the other side, I simply become the younger version of me, the image on the mirror.

Blunt (Erasmus), 5 years old.

I'm back to the exact moment when my friend and neighbor, a devilish kid my age called Jonathan set the doghouse in our backyard on fire, he did this despite my pleads and warnings. I went running to my mom and told her about it. When she asked me who did it, I told her right away. She used the garden house to put out the fire and immediately called Jonathan's mom and informed her about it.

I'm back at the bridge still surrounded by mirrors.

Without thinking I step into another one an instant later.

Blunt (Erasmus), 7 years old.

My friend Johnny cheated on the test by copying the answers from the book. I saw it all with my own eyes. When we were done, he asked me not to tell anyone. I thought about it and asked him to go and tell the teacher what he did. Johnny, you must accept responsibility and request a second chance. He refused so I stopped my friendship with him but never told anyone. Eventually, he was thrown out of the school when he was caught trying to cheat again.

This time when I am back at the bridge, I immediately jump into another mirror.

Blunt (Erasmus,) 10 years old.

One day by accident when visiting my neighbor Ronald, I overheard a conversation between his older brother Patrick and him. Patrick was informing Ronald that their parents could have to sell their house because their father had lost his job. Patrick also said that that they were having difficulties paying for the basic stuff like food and medicines, let alone the utilities like phone, electricity, and water. That night I spoke to my father and explained the situation. In the following days in a discreet way, my father set up several job interviews for Ronald's father, and weeks later he'd found a new job.

Back in the room full of mirrors, I realize that in all the smaller mirrors, the younger images of me are the same as in the larger ones. Basically, I've been to all the mirrors with my image. I turn to the mirror containing many more mirrors. I extend my hand and this time it goes through. Eagerly I walk in. On the other side of it, I run into all my 5 other fellow harlequins who as usual, are all waiting for me. By the expressions on their faces, my fellow harlequins just had similar experiences as mine.

"So, youngsters, what constitutes betrayal?" asks our trusted mentor and antiquarian Morpheus Rubicom, suddenly appearing in front of us.

As usual, he paces back and forth incessantly, filled with nervous energy. His mat of wrangled hair covers part of his face, his lanky features are exacerbated by his hanging loose and ill-fitted clothes.

"I went back to a moment when a friend of mine, Pete, had taken money from the wallet of a schoolmate of ours. Not a friend but someone that went to the same school as ours. Jill struggled at school mainly because she lived far away and had to travel more than 2 hours back and forth from school every day. Her family had economic problems as well, so it was wrong for him to take her money in every sense. I asked Pete to return the money, but he resisted it. I did it for him but that broke our friendship. So, I did not divulge his secret, therefore, did not betray him but that did not prevent me from doing what I thought was the right thing," says Reddish.

"Very well. But what about when our friend's action puts others in danger or is considered a crime?" Asks Mr. Rubicom.

"In that case, there's no betrayal because the person close to us has already betrayed the trust deposited on him or her by breaking the law or putting others in danger.

"That was the case of my friend setting my doghouse on fire," I reply.

"What about when a friend betrays a friend?" Our trusted mentor antiquarian asks.

"Same thing, as it happened with my friend Ronald when I was 10 years old, the family secret I overheard was very private relating to the extreme hardship they were suffering. So, I did not share it with anybody otherwise I would have betrayed him. What I did do was to talk to my father to see if he could assist discreetly so Ronald's father could get a job and he did. But nobody ever knew from me the economic problems they were having," I say.

"Fantastic harlequins, well done, you're almost there," Mr. Rubicom says vanishing in an instant.

"The path ahead of you at some point will be interrupted, it'll be entirely up to you to decide what is the best option ahead of you," says Greenie remembering another one of the clues we earned earlier.

"It is so easy to understand the clues backward when the events have already taken place. We have to learn to visualize them in advance," says a philosophical Reddish.

"The Challenge of Forgiveness"

With a clear path ahead of us we start walking the covered bridge once more. We can see through the sides that the tiny island we are heading to is not that far away. The waters are choppy on the bay.

"Do you see what's coming on the distance ahead of us?" Asks Firee pointing out ominously dark clouds.

"The waters are rising as well," says a skittish Greenie. We pass near another roof ladder into the roof.

"Should we take that and finish this thing walking over the roof?" asks Checkered.

"There's no reason for it. Let's keep on going, we shouldn't be that far away," I say.

Unfortunately, by following my advice we make our FIRST mistake. We walk at a fast pace while the weather continues to deteriorate. The waters where the Grand Canal meets the broad basin of St. Marco are now crashing into the bridge and the water splashes reach the bridge's window level. That's when we see the water trickling into the floor.

"Aqua Alta!" I say. "What?" Asks Breezie.

"This is the super-high tide phenomenon that affects Venice periodically," Firee says.

Water starts pouring in, first through the floor then followed by the walls. With the water level already up to our ankles, Breezie takes charge, "Let's run back to the ladder," he says, and we all start doing so. The water level soon reaches our knees level, and we cannot run any longer but advance pushing the water with our legs. When the water reaches our chests, the movements become even slower. Finally, the water is up to our necks, and everyone is not only anxious and afraid but beginning to panic. We finally see the ladder 20 meters ahead.

"Guys we are going to have to swim for it," I announce.

By the time we reach the ladder the water is already well beyond the walls halfway point. We all get a hold of the ladder and one after the other climb it. Breezie being first pushes the flip-door open and we all make it safely to the roof. The weather is awful. The water is filled with waves that roll directly into the bridge; the water level is not that far off from the roof level.

"We have to get moving," I yell.

Against the wind, we move forward through the roof. But are not advancing. Our destination seems so close and yet so far.

"We have to create a portal to get to the end of the bridge," suggests Reddish.

"We can't do that, we first have to complete this challenge," Firee replies and by doing so we make our SECOND mistake.

The first wave that rolls over us not only knocks the wind out of our lungs but also leaves us soaking wet and cold.

Nobody loses their balance but Firee and Greenie being the lighter of the six of us look wobbly and fragile against these types of weather conditions. The next big wave washes both of them away. I can see the two of them in the water going away in the current.

'C'mon guys do it, use your power,' I think for everyone to hear; otherwise, the howling wind makes it almost impossible to hear each other.

First, we see Greenie hover and I'm about to react and point out the mistake when we see her land back in the water. Right after is Firee who hovers -we can only do it one of us at a time- and picks up Greenie. Steadily they approach us until they land softly on the rooftop. He deposits Greenie delicately down. I get a hold of Greenie and Breezie grabs Firee. Reddish and Checkered hold each other. But all is to no avail. The water level has reached the rooftop.

'Let's dive and go underwater then,' suggests Reddish.

We all agree and jump into the water, by doing so we make our THIRD mistake. The currents are stronger than we could have ever anticipated. We are all thrown in different directions. The only thing certain is that we are going backwards.

'The bridge, dive to the bridge, the passage is all covered by walls, most certainly the currents will be milder or non-existent over there,' Greenie suggests.

'I can't go in any direction, the water is dragging me,' says Checkered.

'Can you go up?' I ask

'I am up on the surface,' she replies.

'Hover and land atop the bridge roof wherever you find a flip door, and dive into the bridge's passage,' I say, 'If any of you is not in the surface, go up to it. Once Checkered is done, let's hover one by one back to the bridge and do the same,' I say addressing the others.

It takes a while, but we all make it into the bridge roof and dive into what's now its submerged covered passage with calm waters. But by following Greenie's advice to dive through it, we make our FOURTH mistake.

'I can see three of you, where's the rest?' Asks Breezie. 'Behind you,' they reply.

There's virtually no current inside the bridge passage. We dive forward with ease and finally make significant progress. But that is about to change in dramatic fashion. Ahead of us, we see a massive wall blocking the way. Once more we are blocked.

'What to do now?' Asks Checkered.

This time none of us knows what to do. We look at each other with eyes of disbelief.

'What about doing the absurd?' Firee asks. 'Like what?' Breezie asks.

'Earlier we talked about it, but one of us dismissed it. We create a portal to take us to the end,' he replies.

We have no better ideas, so we agree and go along with it. A blurry formation appears in the water; eagerly we swim through it, by doing so we make our FIFTH mistake. One that almost costs us the whole quest.

We're just outside of the end of the bridge on dry land. The portal is right in front of us. The seas are totally calm, and the weather is perfect. We turn and realize that we are standing over the small island that houses the Saint Giorgio Maggiore Church, our destination.

"We made it guys," says an enthusiastic Reddish.

"Yeahh," celebrates Firee.

"Wait a minute guys, something's not right," Breezie says.

"It's true; we've not completed our last challenge yet.

Neither have we met with our last antiquarian for any additional questions not gotten her consent that we have successfully gone through the challenge,' reasons Checkered. "She's right. We may have blown or are about to blow all our work," I reflect.

"Without any further move let's attempt to turn back and enter the portal again," says Checkered.

"And go back underwater in front of a blocked passageway, are you crazy?" Says Reddish almost losing it.

"Yes, that's what I'm saying," Checkered says firmly, and taking a step back, she enters and disappears through the portal.

Reluctantly we all follow her. By following what Checkered suggested we have just averted busting out of our quest to become young wizards but have made at the same time our SIXTH mistake. On the other side of the portal, we're all absolutely uncomfortable breathing underwater facing a wall blocking our way, in a seemingly hopeless situation.

We are still lamenting our predicament when the structure around us starts to move and tilt to one side.

'The structure is giving way to the currents. The water is going to wash away the bridge,' I think.

The walls around us start to crack open due to the force of the water stream. A big gap opens on one of the sides. We immediately feel the force of the current trying to pull and drag us.

'I got it, I got it!' Thinks a jubilant Reddish our habitual riddle solver. 'The right step's been right in front of us all the way, but we keep on making mistake after mistake, we could have done it from the very beginning when the water started to come into the bridge passage,' she says.

'What is it Reddish then?' asks an impatient Breezie.

'We create a portal not to the end of the bridge but just before the end of it,' she adds.

The simplicity of it strikes the rest of us. We all look at Reddish with eyes denoting how stupid we all feel. In agreement we all nod, and Reddish creates the portal; we all swim across it and immediately find ourselves in dry land inside the bridge-covered passage. The end of the bridge is just ahead of us. Once more the weather outside is perfect.

"Well, well, well harlequins for a moment I held my breath thinking that you'd blown it all. But you didn't!"

Says Letizia Dillettante the Nordic and statuesque blond mentor and antiquarian. She seems relieved and filled with joy at the same time. "But before we part ways, tell me, what did you learn about forgiveness today?"

We are all kind of lost by her question.

"I don't know about forgiveness in this instance, but we did overcome a series of mistakes by correcting them right away and reaching consensus about constant changes in the course of action," I say.

"That's absolutely right but although each one of you made a crucial error during the challenge, what is it that you never did at any instance?" She presses.

"We didn't waste any time blaming or getting mad at anyone," says proudly Checkered.

"Spot on again. But what is it that you did as well? I give you a hint, it was crucial but not that evident," she says.

This time is Firee who has a huge smile from ear to ear. "We automatically forgave each other after every mistake." No questions asked, no recrimination, no blaming, no anger. We simply applied forgiveness as something implicit all the way," he says with immense satisfaction.

"Harlequins, congratulations! you have successfully completed your last challenge. Go and claim your credentials as young wizards," she says as she swipes her hand and after blowing a warm kiss to each one of us, she vanishes in the air.

We jump up and down in celebration. Hugs, kisses, and relief are all combined in a memorable harlequins pile on.

Hurriedly we exit the bridge and walk into the tiny island where our destination is located, the catwalk serpentines and we have one last view of the water crossing we've just made. Our imaginary and translucent covered bridge has disappeared. On the horizon we see a magnificent rainbow glowing in the distance. We all smile at the sight. It feels like a fitting end to our effort. That's when unexpectedly, a very emotional Checkered starts to recite the last of our clues. And it's dead-on point.

"There's a rainbow at the end of every trying and cumbersome path. Such reward will come to you only if you keep the end in sight and avoid getting sidetracked."

A knot forms in my throat as countless emotions take control of me. I can see that the same is happening to the others. We all know better than anyone the meaning and certitude of the clue we've just heard.

Once we gather ourselves back together, we continue our walk. Ahead we can see our destination, the church of St. Giorgio Maggiore and its connected buildings. Right at the entrance full of energy and enthusiasm stands the object of our fascination, The Orloj, on his right shoulder with one crossed leg sits Thumbpee, Buggie is hovering around like his usual buzzing self.

"Harlequins, you've all graduated with flying colors," he says with a portentous smile, "To become young wizards you've had to work hard to decide when to use your powers. You successfully located each of the antiquarians, this year posing as Shepherd-moors of the clock. You constantly had to figure things out. You made mistakes but corrected them not only rapidly but as important, timely as well. Above all, you did it all without any of the crutches we provided you last year when you were wizard apprentices," he continues, "Both my sons -Thumbpee and Buggie- as you call them have kept me appraised about your accomplishments. I know it wasn't easy. But it wasn't supposed to be, after all, you have now become real wizards -albeit- novices and inexperienced still," he adds in his typical pompous manner, "For this year induction we will go to a very special place, follow me," he says as he starts to walk with his little bouncy steps. Once we are on the way, he swipes his hand, and we are all standing on a now very familiar place: The San Marco Square.

We are standing on the steps that enter the square from the bay area.

"Harlequins, the quay at the water's edge and the steps that follow are called -The Molo. They mark the point of entry in or out of Venice. They are framed by the two 12th century granite columns you see at the end of the steps. The Molo separates the hollow bay called the San Marco basin and the square we are about to enter," explains The Orloj says as he crosses both columns.

"I want to formally welcome you into Venice as Young Wizards. Look at the top of the columns. The grey granite column is San Marco's lion, on top of the red granite column, you can see a man posing as Theodore who was the city's patron until the 9th century," adds the time exacting machine as he delivers our young wizards' credentials right underneath both columns. We high-five each other and celebrate one more time our accomplishment. The Orloj is once again on the march, and we follow. As he walks across the square he has a few parting words, "young wizards, as you can see, your harlequin clothes are gone for good. Next year we're going to meet in the city of light. The quest will be significantly more complex and challenging. The use of your wizard powers will be required at all times. Your goal next time will be to become master wizards. Be aware though, as young wizards you are now exposed to both the good and evil sides of the world of the dark and occult arts. Bad characters may try to get a hold of you. In those cases, it will be solely up to you to defend yourself using everything you've learned in the last two year," he says as we reach the ancient clock's building.

"It's been a pleasure. Now it's time for me to go to rest and hibernate for a while," he says with a little twinkle in his smile.

And just like that the ancient time machine, Thumbpee, and Buggie are gone for another year.

This time the six of us exchange our contact information just in time before everything turns blurry and fuzzy. Once again, we lose sight of the place and time, we are in. At first, I am back inside the San Marco Square astrological clock mechanisms. Slowly I start to see from afar my uncle Bart and aunt Maria Antonella having an animated conversation with Kraus right in front of the ancient clock at San Marco Square.

"Young Erasmus you're back!" he says effusively, "Then my job is done! Take care of yourself. From now on, always keep in mind the words of wisdom just imparted to you by the ancient clock," Zbynek Kraus says and walks away morphing into the old blind man once again.

My aunt and uncle approach me with illuminated faces.

They both hug me for what seems like an eternity.

"What an amazing experience. Lots of fun. It was like a nonstop rollercoaster ride. But I learned so much," I say sighting both satisfied and relieved.

"How do you feel?" Asks my uncle Bartholomeous winking at me.

"Like a brand-new young wizard," is my response before we head back to Milan.

Epilogue

Milan Main Train Station (2031)
(My Parents waiting for me)

Once in town, at the insistence of my uncle Bart, we both sit down with my parents, and I narrate in detail all of the events that took place in Venice. To my surprise they don't express any incredulity towards my story.

"So, you seem to have forgotten that we have a vague idea of what happened to you last year in Prague. As your uncle and aunt did this year, we stayed with Mr. Kraus and while you were out, we were able to see what was going on. When we woke up from the trance we were in, we did remember the highlights of your adventure; and we realized it was true when we corroborated that we were walking back to our hotel about a couple of hours after we met Kraus, but the time and the day were 24 hours later!" Says my father with approving eyes.

With proud eyes my mom says, "Erasmus now you have a new challenge in your hands, it appears that you'll be contending with dangers and risks that you've never experienced before, and this will take place during the ensuing months."

"I'm ready for it, mom," I say outwardly but full of fear and angst deep inside of me.

Shortly after I thank and hug my uncles Maria Antonella and Bart and with teary eyes, I leave the train with my parents. Now I am the chaperone as they resume their summer trip. Our destination is the Orient Express where we'll travel to

Istanbul - the old Constantinople. We'll then take a trip down the Nile River to visit the pyramids and ancient Egyptian temples. Now it's my turn to follow them wherever they want to go on their endless cultural journeys. Time to give them back all the love I receive from them.

The Central Institute of Arts and Literature
(Spring of 2057)

Professor Erasmus Cromwell-Smith finishes his class with a big wide smile for all his students. Massive H.R. screens show shots of all the students attending his class remotely across the nation. He's in for a big surprise though, his girlfriend Laureen Tabernaki is on one of the big screens as she's been watching his last class of the academic year as well. She blows him a kiss and spells the words: "I love you."

"Class, the unforgettable Venice experience taught me lessons that have lasted a lifetime. But after my 2nd adventure, I wasn't even remotely done with my learning curve as a wizard. Next semester I will take you to Paris, the city of light where my third adventure took place with another ancient clock. This time I tried to become a master wizard," he says as he parts ways.

"Enjoy the summer. And that's it for now. This was pure and simply..." He says inviting everyone to second him:

"Insanely awesome!"

Acknowledgment:

Special thanks to D. Suster, Elisa Arraiz, and Tracy-Ann Wynter. Your invaluable help and blind faith on my work have been an intrinsic part of the creation of The Orloj. Also, Daniel Dorse for his masterful work on The Equilibrist series audio books. Thank you all.

About the Author

Erasmus Cromwell-Smith II is an American writer, playwright, and poet. The Orloj series has been crafted through a very intense and intimate introspective dive into the author's own life experiences and wisdom. Volume 3, The Orloj of Paris will be published in the Spring.

www.ingramcontent.com/pod-product-compliance
Lightning Source LLC
Chambersburg PA
CBHW061206210726
48294CB00006B/1772